NEGOTIATED

MARNI MANN

ISBN-13: 978-1720704027

For Ricky.
You fought for this one like a true bestie.
Like usual, you won.

I won this deal. And, lastly, when I told him his demands were bullshit.

I'd responded to everything he'd asked for up until this point.

Now, I was done.

"That won't be necessary," I said. "I'm not coming all the way—"

"The meeting is in two days, Scarlett. In LA. Have your assistant reach out to mine."

Just as I opened my mouth to reply, the phone went dead.

I stared at the screen.

That dickhead had hung up on me.

God, he has balls.

I left my phone on the desk and went down the hall, looking inside each of my partners' offices. The only one here was Brett, so I knocked before I opened his door and poked my head in.

He glanced up from his computer, and I said, "Got a second?"

"Yeah. Of course." He waved me in, and I took a seat across from his desk. "You look like you're about to fuck someone up."

"That would be Hudson Jones."

He pushed back from his desk and crossed his foot over his knee. "Fucking Christ. What's his issue now?"

"He's not bending."

He sighed, shaking his head back and forth. "How far apart are we?"

"Five points."

"That's significant."

ONE

SCARLETT

"SCARLETT DAVIS, I wish you'd just give me what I asked for," Hudson said in a sharp voice once I answered my phone.

I hit Speaker and dropped it onto my desk, my hands returning to my computer to finish the email I'd been typing. "You asked for our most up-to-date numbers."

"I did."

I smiled because it gave me so much satisfaction to say, "And that's what I sent you."

Hudson Jones was an attorney hired by Entertainment Management Worldwide, the management company that The Agency—the business I owned with my three best friends—was partnering with. Once the merger was complete, the actors, athletes, and musicians who were signed with us would then have access to managers in addition to the representation and PR services we currently offered.

That was, if the deal ever went through.

My partners—Brett Young, Jack Hunt, and Max Graham

—and I weren't budging on the terms of the contract. And to show why we didn't have to, this morning, I'd sent Hudson a breakdown of the revenue we'd earned for the previous two months—the amount of time that had passed since he last saw our books. It included Brett's newest client, an actor earning forty-five million a movie, Jack's recently acquired quarterback who was worth one hundred ten million, and the two pop stars Max had signed to labels, worth fifty million each.

"What you gave me was a forecast. There's no way your revenue jumped ten percent in two months."

Conversations like the one we were having used to only take place between Hudson and our attorney. My attorney would then forward me Hudson's questions, write something irrelevant, and bill us an astronomical amount for the two minutes it had taken him to be the middleman.

I'd put a stop to it.

If Hudson wanted something, he would come directly to me.

And, lately, that had been happening all the time.

"Mr. Jones, I'm not a weatherman. I'm an accountant. The last set of figures you received is real; they're not a projection. But what they do is prove that I have no reason to negotiate any of the terms we're requesting."

"Everything is negotiable."

"We both know that isn't true." I crossed my arms over the edge of the desk and then rubbed at the corners of my eyes. "If you'll excuse me, I have to get back to work."

"Scarlett, there are two items still on the table. The percent of equity my clients want and the buyout terms. We've gone over both, and I highly suggest you take the numbers we've offered. They're more than fair."

This fucking guy.

Since the moment he had first called me, there wasn't a single item Hudson and I hadn't argued about. And, before we'd even spoken, our attorney had tried battling it out with him.

I understood the term *hard-ass.*

I was one.

So were my three partners.

We had high expectations that we wanted to be met.

But this man wasn't just a hard-ass. He was quickly becoming the biggest pain in my ass.

"Let me explain this in words you'll understand, Mr. Jones. What we provided was our final offer. If your clients would like to concede, we're ready to sign. If not, we're prepared to walk. Remember, we didn't approach them. They approached us."

A few seconds passed before he said, "We need to talk in person. I'm scheduling a meeting for Thursday."

I glanced toward my computer, clicking on my calendar.

Thursday was two days from now.

And Hudson practiced in LA, which was on the opposite coast as Miami.

"Early afternoon works best," he added. "I'll have my assistant reach out to coordinate your arrival."

While we chatted, which we'd done only twice, I pictured him to be about forty-five, making him fourteen years older than me. I imagined him bald, even more nasally in person, suffering from short-man syndrome with a horrible case of bad breath.

Once I had his description locked down, I'd envisioned his expression when I told him we weren't caving and again when

"Brett, it's what we deserve. Every calculation I've made proves it. Our attorney even agrees."

The heel of his shoe started clinking against the edge of his desk. "We either need to get this wrapped up or squash the deal. But the lawyers are dragging this out, and every day that passes, they make more goddamn money off of us."

I knew how much our attorney would earn off this partnership, and it made me sick to my stomach.

"Hudson wants me to go to LA and meet with him on Thursday."

"For what?"

I shrugged. "I assume he wants us to come to an agreement."

His eyes moved to his computer, and he used his mouse to click on the screen. "I'll be in New York on Thursday."

"I know. Max will be in Vegas, and Jack will be in Atlanta, so none of you are available to go with me."

"What about our attorney?"

I'd thought about this same thing as I walked down the hall toward his office.

"I don't think I'll need him. I won't be there to sign anything; I'll be there to talk."

"No, you'll be there to fucking battle."

I smiled. "Precisely."

"Get what you want, get him to agree, and get this deal done."

I hadn't expected to close out the final round of negotiations. But, since the very beginning, I had taken the lead on this merger. It'd started when the three owners of Entertainment Management Worldwide—Jayson Brady, Blake Hunter, and Shane Walker—reached out through email. They'd expressed their interest, and after a bit of research, I'd decided to meet with them. Once I'd had a better understanding of what they were looking for, I'd pitched the idea to my partners.

At first glance, the contract they'd provided looked pretty decent. But, once I'd begun to dig into the numbers and break them down, I had known we needed much more.

That was four months ago.

And it still felt like we were miles apart.

"This is the last chance," Brett warned. "I'm not going another round with them, and neither are you."

By end of day Thursday, I'd know if we were going to gain a partnership that would net us millions, making us the highest-grossing agent and management firm in the country, or if all the hard work I'd put in would be for nothing.

It was all coming down to me.

The only partner who didn't negotiate for a living.

Instead, I was the chief financial officer. I'd been working behind the scenes since the day we opened the business. But I'd grown up with these guys, I'd gone to college with them, I'd lived with them for years, and we'd spent our entire career together.

In that time, I'd learned how to hold my own.

So, if Hudson thought I would just lie on my back and take whatever he gave me in Thursday's meeting, then he'd read me all wrong.

Personally, I liked that position when it involved a headboard and handcuffs.

But, when it came to my job and the livelihood of my partners, I was the dominant one.

Soon, he would see that side of me.

I stood from the chair and moved behind it. "I'll make the right decision for all of us. Don't worry; I won't disappoint."

"You never have."

TWO

HUDSON

I WAS AT MY DESK, working on an email, when my office line began to ring. I checked the screen at the top of the phone and saw that it was my assistant calling, so I hit the Speaker button and said, "Yes?"

"Everything is all set up, Mr. Jones. I've spoken with my contacts in both of the places that we discussed, and they promise to give you whatever information you want."

I pulled back the black diamond cuff link to check my watch. The platinum hands on the Rolex showed it would be several more hours until her contacts needed to come through. If they didn't, they weren't getting a dime from me. Neither was my assistant because her ass would be fired by the morning.

"I want to be notified the second your contacts hear or see anything. Do you hear me?"

"My phone won't be leaving my hand until you get what you're looking for."

I took my fingers off the keyboard and looked toward my

office door where I knew she was sitting only a few feet away. "Tina?"

"Yes, Mr. Jones?"

"Don't fuck this up."

I hung up, and my inbox showed a new email had come through. It was from my client, Jayson Brady, one of the owners of Entertainment Management Worldwide, who was in the process of partnering with The Agency.

Hudson,
Do whatever you have to do to get this deal done. I want the
terms agreed upon and the contract signed by next week.
—Jayson

I had a week.

So, it was a good thing I had a hell of a plan.

Jayson, Blake, and Shane had known what they were doing when they hired me.

They wanted the best.

And that was what they were getting.

———

Six hours later, I was in the private restroom in my office, putting on the gray suit my assistant had picked out. Once I had my shirt tucked in and a tie resting down my chest, I took in the whole outfit.

Jesus Christ.

Fucking twenty-something-year-olds.

They didn't know anything about men's fashion.

If I asked Tina how to post on a goddamn social media site,

she'd have that handled in seconds. But ask her to match a suit and tie, and you'd think she was fucking color blind.

Shaking my head, I said to her, "Give me a better tie," while she stood outside my door. "The one you chose looks like shit with the gray."

"How about—"

"Give me a black one," I said, cutting her off.

The door opened, and she handed me a solid black tie made of silk.

I wrapped it around my neck, and after approving of the way it looked, I got started on the Windsor knot.

"The SUV has arrived," she said from the doorway. "I'm just waiting for confirmation from my contacts, and then you'll be on your way."

I was staring at her from the mirror, watching her shift her weight between both feet, her hands fidgeting at her sides.

This was the part of her job she didn't like.

The things that happened off the clock.

Still, she was a decent assistant. She just couldn't hide her emotions, so it was a good fucking thing I never had to bring her to the courtroom.

I checked the time on my wrist. "I can't believe your contacts don't know anything yet. It's almost nine o'clock."

She pointed at the cell phone that she was squeezing between her fingers. "I'll call them again. Can I get you anything before I close this door?"

"You can hurry up."

As she left, I finished looping my tie through, and then I slipped on my jacket. I took a few steps closer to the mirror and checked my hair, making sure the gel was where it needed to be and that my stubble wasn't longer than a day's worth. I grabbed some cologne off the shelf and sprayed my neck. Just as I was setting it back, there was a knock at the door.

Tina opened it and said, "Here's the address, Mr. Jones." She held out her hand, and there was a small piece of paper resting on her palm.

I took it from her and read what she had written, eventually glancing up. "This can't be right."

"My contacts verified it."

The address wouldn't be known by everyone. But I'd lived in LA for the thirty-eight years I'd been alive, so I knew what went down in this town. And I knew what went down at 555 Pine Street.

"Do you know what this place is?" I asked.

She nodded; her expression told me she wasn't comfortable discussing it. "Will you be able to get in, or do I need to make a phone call?"

Even though I knew all about it, I'd never been inside.

"Make the phone call," I told her. "But make sure you speak to Leanna. She'll get things handled."

Her cheeks flushed.

She wanted to die of embarrassment.

It was also a good thing that I didn't find her attractive because she'd never survive in my bedroom.

"I'll be back in a few minutes," she said.

As she shut the door, I went over to the toilet and dropped the piece of paper into the water. The blue ink ran and swirled around the bowl as I flushed it.

The last fucking thing I needed was someone to see that in my trash and spread rumors all over town.

But what I'd done stopped that, and the trail ended here

since my assistant, her contacts, and anyone at 555 Pine Street were under contract and couldn't say anything.

I stepped out of the restroom, and as I was moving toward the closet, Tina came into my office.

"I paid the fee and gave them all the information they'd asked for. When you get there, you're going to have to sign an NDA. Other than that, you're all set." Her skin was even redder. "Is there anything else you need, Mr. Jones?"

"Go home." When she started following my instruction, I added, "You did good today."

She dipped her head and closed the door behind her.

555 Pine Street, I thought.

This wasn't how I'd thought I'd be spending my night.

But, fuck, I couldn't have planned it any better.

THREE

SCARLETT

I SAT in the back of the SUV I'd hired for the night, the driver weaving through the traffic in downtown LA. Over the last six months, it was a city I had been finding myself spending more and more time in. That was due to the office we'd built here, The Agency expanding into the market where the four of us had begun our careers. But, over the past few weeks, my trips to the West Coast had died down. Max was now managing things here, and all the staff had been hired. They were operating smoothly, and they just didn't need me.

Ironically, I found myself missing LA whenever I returned to Miami.

Brett and Jack hated it here and wanted to live in South Florida.

But Max had recently relocated here to be with his girlfriend, Eve Kennedy, an extremely successful stylist who dressed most of Hollywood.

I was the only single one in our group after breaking things off with the quarterback from Miami. Vince Hedman was extremely attractive, loyal, and sweet. He was just too soft.

I didn't want a teddy bear in bed.

I wanted someone who showed dominance, who could get my attention and keep it, whose commands would make me obey.

Without it, my needs just weren't met.

Vince had had to go.

Right after I'd left him, we'd started building the second location and negotiating a possible partnership between The Agency and Entertainment Management Worldwide. I was growing our finance department, so it could handle double, maybe triple, the amount of work.

I was busier than I'd ever been.

I needed a release.

And I didn't have time to look for someone to give me one.

So, when my best friend, Pepper Michaels, had suggested I stop by her sex club, Lush, to get what I needed, I'd realized how perfect this opportunity was. The club was exclusive. To be granted a membership, you had to go through a lengthy approval process. Only Miami's top elite was allowed in, and the same was true for her LA location. There were rules, a dress code, and a two-year waiting list to join.

I wasn't looking to jump into a relationship again.

I wanted someone who could fuck me the way I needed to be ravaged.

A place where I could lose myself in pleasure instead of agonizing over the stress at work.

Because, while I was at work, I constantly had to be in charge. I had to make all the decisions. I had to manage and dictate and delegate.

So, when it came to sex, I wanted to be controlled.

It was a balance.

One that had become extremely important in my life.

In the days leading up to going, I had found myself fantasizing about the stranger who would touch my body, who would give me exactly what I needed without any attachment or expectations after the two of us came.

Because my membership gave me access to both locations, I usually visited the LA spot when I was in town.

That was where the SUV was pulling up to now.

The driver opened my door, and as I climbed out of the backseat, I said, "I'm going to be several hours. Please park out back and wait for me there."

He nodded, and I headed toward the entrance.

As I reached it, I knocked twice. A security guard answered, holding a tablet that he extended in my direction. I placed my hand on top of it, and I watched it scan my prints to confirm my identity. When the screen turned green, I pulled my arm back.

"Miss Davis," the security guard said, checking the tablet before he looked at me again. "Welcome."

"Thank you."

Once inside, there was a reception area where several women, wearing masks and lingerie, were standing around a large desk. Their role was to greet guests, get them whatever they needed, and make sure they were comfortable.

"We're glad to have you back, Miss Davis," one of them said as she walked over to me. "Can I escort you to the bar and get you something to drink?" By the way the feathers were weaved into her hair, she reminded me of a peacock.

"I'm fine. Thank you."

She continued to follow me until we reached the set of doors that were on the far side of the room. This was what separated the chamber—the main area of the sex club—from the entrance, and it also added another layer of security.

We both stopped, and I glanced at her.

"Enjoy your evening," she said, and she turned her head and nodded at the security guard who stood at the desk.

That was the signal for him to unlock the door, and it started to slide open. When there was a gap large enough for me to fit through, I stepped into the chamber.

Sex.

That was the only thing that came to mind as I stood on the other side. It was all I could see—not just the act, although that was certainly happening in here, but there were hints of sex everywhere. Erotic scents floated in the air. The decorations and wall textures and furniture were all done in sensual colors, and the fabrics were made of leather and satin and velvet. And then there were the sounds—floggers slapping bare skin, handcuffs clinking against metal spokes, moans in every level and tone.

The chamber was a half-circle with hallways darting off the arc. Each hallway contained several rooms. Some were private and locked for anyone who didn't want an audience. The others didn't have doors. But all of them were equipped with props to cover an array of fetishes.

The center of the circle was where people gathered when they first arrived. It was where you could grab a drink and something to eat. There were couches and high-top tables and low-playing music. Conversations were held; they just happened quietly. No one wanted to talk over the moaning and screaming that filled the background.

Since tomorrow was all about business—going to battle against Hudson Jones—I didn't want tonight to be about talking. I wanted to relax. To release the pent-up tension.

I wanted to lose myself.

So, I didn't stop in the circle and sit on one of the couches or grab a drink at the bar.

I went to one of my favorite spots, which was the hallway to the far right, and then I stopped at the last room on the left.

There was no door on this one.

Instead, it had a large archway, and in the center was a four-poster bed. Usually, a woman was on one of the sex swings in here or on the Saint Andrew's Cross, and I found that so incredibly seductive. But, tonight, there was a woman spread across the middle of the mattress with a rope wrapped around each ankle and wrist, and then those were tied to the wooden posters.

She was naked.

Kneeling on the bed was a man in a suit. He was holding a riding crop and tapping it on her nipples. Every time the leather hit her skin, my legs would press together. That gave me just enough friction to alleviate the tingles that pulsed through my clit.

I wanted the slapping sensation on my body.

I wanted the rope to burn my wrists.

I wanted to feel the restraint from being bound to the bed.

He moved the crop down the center of her breasts and dragged it across the top of her pussy.

When she screamed, which was the neediest sound I'd ever heard, the softest moan came out of my lips. My fingers clasped the edge of the doorway, nails digging into the molding.

I understood where that need came from. How just a brush of leather across her clit would give her a little of what her body was craving.

I throbbed for her.

For the crop.

For a flick between my thighs.

"What would you sound like if I tied you to that bed?" a man asked from behind me.

His voice was rich and deep, and I could tell he was close to me.

I immediately turned around, hoping his face was just as sexy.

Our stares locked, and I felt my lips pull into a smile.

He wasn't just sexy.

This man was absolutely gorgeous.

He was around six foot four inches with black hair that was tousled to the side and piercing green eyes.

He said nothing as he gazed at me, obviously waiting for me to respond.

"I would be louder than her," I eventually said.

His eyes dipped down my body. With each inch, I felt my breathing start to speed up. Because, as he took in more, so did I.

His Tom Ford suit.

Those large, masculine hands.

A body that seemed incredibly fit.

And, oh God, that handsome face.

I could picture it between my legs.

I could feel the control melting at my feet.

"Would you be still?" he asked. "Or would I have to tie the rope so tightly, it would burn your skin?"

My ankles stung in response.

I didn't hate the feeling.

"That depends."

His brows rose, and it produced deep grooves across his forehead and crinkles at the sides of his eyes.

"On what?" he asked.

And, when he spoke, my attention was drawn to his lips. They were thick, and they appeared so soft. The thought of them surrounding my nipple was beginning to make me squirm.

"If you ordered me to sit still or if you ordered me to fight the ropes."

He looked at my mouth for several seconds before those inviting eyes moved back up to mine. "What's your name?"

"Scarlett." I held my hand out, and he clasped it. The strength in his fingers didn't go unnoticed. I could practically feel them plunging inside me. "And you are?"

"Andrew." He released my hand before setting his on my shoulder and turning me toward the bed. "Tell me something, Scarlett."

Another jolt burst through my clit as I watched the crop come down on her inner thigh.

Andrew's mouth then went to the shell of my ear, and he said in his growly voice, "Do you want an audience, or do you want us to be alone?"

Us.

He lifted the long strands of hair resting over my chest, and he moved them behind my back. Goose bumps covered me the second I felt his touch, and they grew across my skin as his fingers left me.

I looked across my shoulder, giving him only my profile. "I didn't come here to answer questions."

I wanted that privilege to be taken away from me.

And it suddenly was as he clasped my hand between his fingers, and then he used that same hand to lead me down the hallway.

FOUR

HUDSON

NOTHING COULD BREAK MY CONCENTRATION. Not even the woman screaming in the background as she got slapped with a riding crop. That was because I was staring at Scarlett's face, waiting for her to realize it was me and flip the fuck out.

But that didn't happen.

As it turned out, she had no idea who I was.

I was surprised she had given me her real name. I hadn't expected that from this place. If it was something Scarlett did, I imagined everyone else was just as honest.

Even though she and I'd never met, I was sure she would have looked me up. At the very least, to just get a sense of whom she'd be facing during tomorrow's meeting.

She obviously hadn't because she gazed right back like I wasn't the attorney representing the opposition in the deal we'd been negotiating for months.

To double-check, I gave her my middle name and waited once again for it to all click into place.

It didn't.

So, I tried one last time, taking a few steps toward her, grazing my hand across her shoulder. I thought my touch would cause a little resistance, that it would get her mind straight, and maybe there would be some recognition.

There was none.

Just a feral look in her eyes that told me her pussy was already wet.

It was a look that surprised the fuck out of me.

I hadn't expected for her to be so responsive, to not know who I was, to not be pissed as hell that I had come here to see her. I'd imagined that I'd have to cool her down and feed her a few cocktails and a heavy dose of charm before I could get her to talk to me.

This outcome was so much better.

She was letting me right in.

And inside her was a place I'd fucking love to be.

There wasn't a man on this planet who wouldn't want to trade places with me. Scarlett was the most gorgeous woman in this club, even more beautiful than a majority of the celebrities her company represented.

I was one lucky bastard.

And, now, I had this goddamn piece of perfection squeezing my fingers while I led her to a private room.

When I'd first arrived, I'd familiarized myself with the layout in here, so I knew where I needed to take Scarlett, and that was toward the center of the main room. I then led her down a hallway, and I unlocked the last door on the right, using the key from my pocket.

Once she'd figured out who I was, my plan had been to bring her in here to talk.

But fucking was so much hotter than talking.

When I opened the door, Scarlett walked inside first. Her hand slid out of mine, and she stopped at the base of the bed and turned around to face me.

I stayed in the back of the room, my hands resting on the armoire behind me.

If she didn't come here to answer questions, then she came to lose control. I could tell that was what she wanted by the way she'd stared at the riding crop, how her body had swayed each time the leather came down on the girl's skin. Instead of flinching, she'd appeared more turned on with each strike.

So, that was what she'd get in here.

A total loss of control.

In more ways than fucking one.

"You need a safe word," I said.

"Cherry." She smiled as she said it.

It obviously came with memories.

None would be as sexy as the ones I was about to give her.

"What are your limitations, Scarlett?"

She turned her face. Now, there was just a hint of her grin left. "If I can't handle what you're giving me, I'll use the safe word."

I was fine with that. I just needed to know she could get me to stop.

Now, she could.

"I want you to leave your dress right there." I pointed at the floor in front of her. "If you have anything on underneath, place it on the nightstand. Then, get on the bed."

She pushed her ass against the mattress and reached behind her back. Her dress began to loosen as she pulled down the zipper, and eventually, it fell to the ground.

That fucking body.

I couldn't take my eyes off of it.

She was flawless.

Not too skinny or too fit, but someone who certainly took care of herself and maintained her curves at the same time.

I had known whatever was under that dress would be exceptional.

But I hadn't anticipated this.

She stepped out of the material and reached behind her back once more to unhook her strapless bra. As she peeled it off her chest, my cock ground against the zipper of my pants.

She was natural, no bigger than a handful.

And fucking stunning.

Her panties dropped down her long legs, and she lifted them into her hand, walking them over to the nightstand.

I growled as she placed them on the wooden top, and I hissed the reminder, "Get on the fucking bed."

With her eyes still on me, she crawled onto the center and knelt.

I didn't give her another order because I wanted to take her in.

So, my stare slowly dragged over every inch of her skin. "So fucking perfect," I roared.

It was skin I needed to touch.

A body I needed to devour with my mouth.

A pussy I needed to feel around my cock.

I no longer cared who she was or why I was here or the conversation I was supposed to be having with her.

Only one thing mattered, and that was giving her what she wanted.

"Get on your back," I said, and I moved over to the side of

the bed. As I watched her obey, I lifted the panties into my hand and brought them up to my nose, inhaling her scent and groaning, "Fuck, that smells good."

I hadn't thought it was possible for tonight to get any better.

I was wrong.

Because never in my life had I inhaled anything as sexy as Scarlett's cunt.

I slipped the panties into my pocket and opened the drawer on the nightstand. Since I'd inventoried the room before she arrived, checking out the paraphernalia that was available, I knew there were silk scarves in here. I grabbed four and wrapped the first one around the top-right poster of the bed. Then, I looped it around her wrist and tied it to the wood. I did the same to her other wrist and both ankles until her body was stretched across the whole bed.

I knew there were toys in the other drawers and more in the armoire. But, tomorrow, when Scarlett walked into my office and made the connection, there was a good chance my hands would never be on her again.

So, tonight, I was going to use them as much as I could.

I stuck two fingers into my mouth to wet them, and then I dropped them onto her nipple. "Mmm," I breathed.

"Andrew," she gasped as I pinched it and tugged.

I wasn't gentle.

I wanted her to feel a quick burst of pain that I followed up with pleasure, caressing the end with long strokes from my thumb.

Her moan halted when I tightened around her again, and it deepened when I released.

I wasn't sure which one she liked more, so I tried squeezing harder and adding spit when I lightly brushed over it.

Every motion earned me a verbal response.

And every one sounded as though she was feeling incredible.

I leaned onto the edge of the bed to get closer to her tits, and then I held my hand right next to it and flicked her nipple with my finger.

Her scream was short and extremely sharp.

I let the pain simmer before I blew air across it.

It was already hard and puckered, but the skin around it seemed to tighten even more. Then, her mouth opened, and the back of her head ground into the bed.

"You like it when I blow on your fucking tits," I said.

Because she hadn't asked, I gave her another burst of it.

Her ankles pulled against the scarves, trying to stretch the knots and get free. "Please," she cried right before I flicked her again.

She wanted something, and begging was the only way she could ask for it.

But, at this moment, I owned her pleasure. I controlled what she got and when it would happen.

I leaned a little further onto the bed, and I bit the top of her right tit. "Yes," I groaned as the taste of her flesh filled my mouth.

I wasn't as hard on her as I could have been. But it was enough to catch her off guard, for her back to straighten, for her to still be feeling the sting several seconds later.

Her eyes told me she wanted me to do it again.

Such a goddamn submissive.

I wondered what had made her this way.

As I continued to search her eyes, that answer came to me.

When Scarlett stepped inside this club, she no longer had to be the boss. She also didn't have to do any training. This place was a breeding ground for dominance, and the men in here knew what they were doing.

Coming here was more like coming home.

And, although I wasn't a regular, she didn't need to worry about me. I knew the language of dominance. It was a lifestyle I practiced. And I knew I could make her feel better than she ever had.

As I blew on her, her ankles strained against the ties, her knees pointing inward in an attempt to push them together.

She was trying to put pressure on her pussy.

It was feeling lonely.

I'd fix that soon.

I took in another breath and blew out the air in one fast exhale. The skin around her nipple tightened, and goose bumps spread over her skin.

She liked that.

I knew she'd like this even more.

I reached down and whipped just the tips of my fingers across her pussy.

"Fuck," I hissed as my hand left her skin. "You're so wet."

I wasn't even inside her, yet the part I'd touched near her lips was soaked.

I hadn't expected her to be that turned on.

But it was so sexy.

When I did it again, I went slower, my finger sliding onto her clit while my other hand slapped the top of it.

"Yes!" she screamed. "Please give me more."

Hearing her beg for me was so fucking hot.

FIVE
SCARLETT

I WASN'T sure how long I'd been strapped to this bed. There weren't any clocks inside the chamber. Time didn't exist while you were in here. At least, it certainly felt that way when Andrew's hands were all over me.

It wasn't all pleasure that he had given me. There was plenty of pain, too.

I loved both.

It was foreplay.

But I had a feeling he was about to give me more because he was now at my feet, loosening the scarves. When the knots were out, I felt the indentations the material had left on my skin from all the tension I'd caused.

Or Andrew had caused.

Every time he'd touched me, my legs had strained, forcing the scarves to dig into me.

And, now, I was doing the same to my wrists as I waited for him to undo those.

But he didn't move.

He stayed by the center of the bed and stared at my body.

It was such a turn-on to watch the hunger grow in his eyes.

He was a stranger.

But, in here, that didn't matter.

It was about control, being satisfied. It was about finding a release in a place where I felt comfortable.

Those were the things that kept me coming back.

The men in here were typically attractive. Pepper made sure of that. But I hadn't seen a man as handsome as Andrew.

God, he was better-looking than anyone I'd ever dated.

"You're beautiful," he said, his gaze slowly moving up my body until it stopped on my face.

"Untie me, please. I want to touch you."

I needed to know what he looked like under his shirt. If he was as built as he appeared, if his skin was soft, if he had any hair on his body.

"Untie you," he repeated, a smile covering his face as he laughed.

He took off his jacket, setting it on the sex swing behind him. He then reached for his tie and loosened it just a little. Each movement caused his button-down to tighten, showing me the size of his muscles, the broadness of his shoulders, the hard-on that I could see pushing into his pants.

I couldn't wait for him to get naked, so I moaned, "Please."

My stare was on his cock, wishing the zipper would drop and it would spring out toward my mouth.

"Is this what you want?" His hand dipped down over his suit pants, and he grabbed his cock. With his fingers around it, I could see how large the bulge was, the entire length, the way his whole hand fit around it.

My God.

"Yes," I admitted, "I want that." As I looked up toward his face, I felt myself gnawing on my lip.

He climbed onto the bed and slid down my body until he knelt between my legs. "That was for you."

"You mean, the way your hands touched me?"

He nodded. "Now, this part is for me."

I expected him to drop his pants, slip on a condom, and plunge his cock inside me.

He circled his hands around my thighs instead, and he spread them apart. His face lowered until it was inches above my pussy, and then he glanced up at me from in between my legs. "You won't need your hands for a while, so they can stay right where they are."

Just as I was about to respond, his mouth surrounded my clit, and he growled, "Jesus, you taste so goddamn good."

The way he licked me caused my back to shoot off the mattress and arch, for my toes to dig into the bed. "Fuck yes," I gasped, completely overwhelmed by the sensation and the way his two fingers were now diving in and out of me.

His tongue was fast.

But it wasn't just his speed that caused me to buck against his mouth.

It was the way he used only the tip to flick across the most sensitive part of my body. It was the thickness of his fingers and how he swiveled them inside me, pulling out to his knuckles and gliding back in. It was the sounds he made as he ate me, noises that told me he was enjoying this as much as I was.

Andrew was no amateur.

This man ate pussy like it was his favorite thing to do.

And the way he was going at me told me he wanted me to come.

It only took a few more seconds, and then I groaned, "*Ahhh.*"

My stomach shuddered, and my legs tightened on the sides of his face. Pleasure was spreading throughout my whole body, and I rocked my hips back and forth to ride out the rest of the orgasm.

"That's what I wanted," he hissed.

I expected him to still and then stop. To hear the crinkle of the foil. For my body to instantly be filled in an entirely different way.

It didn't happen.

Because the man wasn't done feeding on me.

His face stayed right where it was, surrounding my clit with the flatness of his tongue, keeping his fingers all the way inside me while he ground them around in a circle.

"Andrew," I panted, once again completely immersed in his movements, each one making me feel even more lost.

"I need to taste you for a little longer."

The sound of his voice.

The desire, the hunger.

All so incredibly hot.

"You can stay there for as long as you want," I told him.

And then I let out a moan as he sucked my clit into his mouth, his tongue mashing the edge, and the build immediately returned. This time, my legs shook. My hips pumped up and down, working the sensation through my body.

"Oh God!" I shouted, the pulsing moving into my stomach, causing it to quiver.

He finally released my clit and slowed, now giving me

long, hard strokes across my entire pussy. "Mmm. You taste so fucking sweet when you come."

His nose was pressed into the top of my entrance, and I watched him breathe me in.

"Let me taste your cum."

Our eyes locked as I stared down at him.

I wanted his cock in my mouth, his tip banging against the back of my throat.

I wanted to run my tongue along the vein on the back side and across the small slit at the head.

I wanted him dripping down my throat.

He released my thighs. Then, he stood and said, "Not tonight."

His response surprised me, so I had to confirm I'd heard him correctly. "You're not going to fuck me?"

He grabbed his jacket from the sex swing, sliding his arms through it, and he straightened his tie. He then moved to the top of the bed and began to loosen the remaining two scarves.

One arm dropped and then the other. I brought them up to my chest and took turns rubbing them.

Even though the material hadn't left a mark, I'd be sore for at least a day. The same was true for my ankles.

"Get dressed," he said, and he went over to the armoire and pushed his back against it.

I climbed off the mattress and put my bra on first. My heels were next, and then I wrapped both hands around one of the bed posters. "I think you have something of mine."

He smiled.

It was beautiful.

Charming.

Unbelievably enticing.

"You're not getting the panties back."

I reached down and picked up the dress, stepping into it and zipping the back. "Oh no?"

He was now holding the panties, rubbing his thumb around the fabric the same way it had traced my skin. "Let's go get a drink."

Before I could respond, he was opening the door, clasping my hand, and leading me toward the bar.

There were two bartenders. Both were men. They were dressed in just a pair of suit pants with suspenders that clung around their bare shoulders, and there were masks on their faces.

Pepper didn't want the members to hook up with the staff, so it was required that they hide their identity.

When we reached the bar top, one of the guys approached us and said, "What can I get you, Mr. Jones?"

Jones?

"That's your last name?" I asked Andrew.

Andrew Jones.

I didn't recall him saying it earlier; we'd both just used our first names.

He nodded, and then he looked at the bartender. "Whiskey on the rocks." He glanced back at me. "What do you drink?"

"Vodka, the same way," I told the both of them. I had Andrew's full attention, and his stare was just as hungry as before. "Tell me something about yourself, Andrew. Like why you let my ankles out of the scarves."

"Because I knew I'd like the way your thighs felt against my face."

Tingles started to spread up my neck, and I tried rubbing it away with my fingers. "And my hands?"

"I didn't want you to push me away."

"You think I would have stopped you from licking me?"

"I didn't want to take the chance."

I leaned the side of my body into the bar. "Let me tell you something about me, Andrew. I always want more."

"Even now?"

I paused for a second and finally said, "Yes."

"You're insatiable."

"And you're not? You didn't even get off tonight."

He bent his neck, his mouth moving closer to my ear. "I got to feel you come on my tongue. I got to taste it and swallow it. That's as good as getting off."

I felt the wetness start to move between my lips.

I needed to know more about this handsome man.

"What do you do?" I asked him.

The bartender placed two glasses in front of us. Andrew took the drinks, and I followed him over to a high-top that gave us a little more privacy.

I gripped the vodka and took a sip.

"I work with businesses," he eventually said after swallowing some of his whiskey.

"In what capacity?"

"One that will bore you." His hand lowered and reached around the table until it found my waist. I was surprised by how much I enjoyed his touch. "How often do you come here?"

"Not very often, and that's because I don't live here."

"No?"

My chest hammered away from the intensity of his gaze. "I live in Miami."

"Do you—"

But his voice cut off when a woman walking by stopped at our table. From the way she was dressed, I knew she was a member, not an employee.

She stood right next to him and said, "In all my life, I never thought I'd see *the* Hudson Jones at Lush."

Hudson Jones?

As in the attorney for Entertainment Management Worldwide?

There was no way this was happening.

He wouldn't have done this just because we were on opposing sides, because we wanted different numbers.

Would he really go this far?

As I answered my own question, my entire body began to shake.

Hudson stared at me while he responded, "Cindy, I'll give you a call tomorrow."

I released the vodka and gripped the side of the table with both hands, waiting until she left before I spoke, "Tell me she didn't just call you Hudson Jones." I kept my voice low, so I wouldn't cause a scene.

Something I'd never do in Pepper's place of business.

"That's my name, Scarlett."

Fucking asshole.

"But you told me your name was Andrew." I took a step back, and his hand dropped from my waist. "You lied to me. You're the goddamn attorney representing Jayson, Blake, and Shane." A loathing began to pour its way into my throat. "Did you plan this?"

His expression didn't deny it, nor did he say a word.

"My God, you did. You set this whole thing up." My brain wouldn't stop trying to piece this all together, to make sense of why he was here. And then it clicked. "You want to blackmail me, don't you? You want to get something that you can use against me. That you can hold over my head, so I'll agree to your terms. And, now, you have all the information you need."

I felt sick to my stomach.

"Listen to me—"

Listen to him?

"You're a disgusting piece of shit with zero morals and even less integrity."

Eating the pussy of the woman he was negotiating a multi-million-dollar deal with. As far as I was concerned, that was a whole new level of low.

And I'd fallen for it.

He'd had a motive.

To put his hands and mouth on my body to get what he wanted. Not just in the private room, but also in the deal we were supposed to work out in his office tomorrow.

I'd never felt more blindsided.

Or betrayed.

"Scarlett, let me explain—"

"That chance is long gone." He reached for me, and I took another step back. "Stay the fuck away from me."

There was so much more I wanted to say. I just wouldn't disrespect Pepper that way, so I turned around and weaved my way through the rest of the chamber and toward the front of the building.

"Scarlett," I heard him say behind me.

He said my name two more times before I got through the

door and into the reception area. Hurrying through that small space, I avoided the employees who were trying to approach me to make sure I'd had a good night. Once I got outside, I went to the parking lot and climbed into the back of the SUV.

"Would you like to go to the hotel?" the driver asked as he turned around in his seat.

"Yes," I told him.

I retrieved my clutch that I'd hidden in the seat pocket and grabbed my phone from inside, pulling up the flight schedule for the company's private plane. It was completely booked, and it couldn't pick me up until my previously arranged time.

That was two days from now.

Flying commercial was an option; it just meant the guys would ask why I had come home early.

What the hell am I going to say to them?

I couldn't think that far ahead.

With the phone still in my hand, I pulled up a blank email, addressed it to our attorney, and began to type.

The last time we spoke, I made our offer extremely clear.

It hasn't changed.

Don't call me unless the contract is ready to be signed.

You have one week.

Never again would I deal with Hudson Jones.

All communication would now take place between our attorneys.

His mouth had fucked me once.

I would make sure it never happened again.

SIX

HUDSON

WHEN I GOT to my house in the Hollywood Hills, I dropped my keys on the table by the front door and went straight to the bar. I didn't bother with any ice. I just poured the whiskey into a short glass and shot it into my mouth. Once the back of my throat stopped burning, I drained several more fingers' worth, the fire on my tongue immediately returning.

Goddamn it, tonight hadn't gone the way I'd planned.

Blackmail her?

That wasn't my intention because, before she'd arrived at Lush, never for a fucking second had I thought she wouldn't know who I was. So, what I had been worried about was her flipping her shit on me. Getting the chance to touch her body had never crossed my mind.

Then, things had just gotten worse.

She'd walked out without giving me a chance to explain.

She'd come to her own conclusion, one that could jeopardize all the work I'd put into this deal for Entertainment

Management Worldwide. And her theory couldn't be more wrong.

But I couldn't have chased her. Not when there was a chance she'd air her assumptions in front of the entire room, and anyone who might have heard would get the wrong impression. Especially when I already knew half of the goddamn people there.

I had a reputation to uphold in this town.

I wasn't about to fuck that up.

So, I'd let her go, knowing I would handle this in the morning before she got out of town since I highly doubted she'd be coming to my office.

Somehow, I would fix this.

I took out my phone and hit the number that connected me to Tina.

She answered, "Good evening, Mr. Jones."

"I want the name of the hotel that Scarlett is staying in and the room number. And I want all of that texted to me by six o'clock tomorrow morning."

"Okay, but—"

I disconnected the call and slammed my phone on the bar top.

Scarlett's pussy had tasted so fucking delicious tonight. Her body had felt so good underneath my hands. Her hips had pumped so hard as she rode my goddamn face. The way she had felt when she convulsed around my fingers was perfect.

But none of that mattered.

Because, at this moment, she hated me.

And I needed to change that.

The following morning, Tina texted me at ten minutes before six, and she sent all the information I'd asked for. The only thing she didn't know was if Scarlett was still at the hotel. Her source didn't start her shift until eight, so I'd be blind for the next two hours.

I called Scarlett at six.

And then again at seven.

She didn't answer either time, and I didn't leave a voice message. She was likely not going to listen to it, so after I hung up the second time, I opened her last text box, and I began to type.

Me: We need to talk.

Me: At least let me explain myself, Scarlett.

Me: If you keep ignoring me, I'm going to come to your hotel.

Scarlett: Like I told my attorney last night, all correspondence must now go through him. I won't accept texts, emails, or phone calls from you, your assistant, or your three clients. Please delete my number.

Me: I'll be at your room in fifteen minutes. Answer the goddamn door when I knock.

Scarlett: I've already checked out...asshole.

Jesus fucking Christ.

I left my phone on the kitchen counter and walked to the patio before I threw my cell through the goddamn glass door.

When it came to business, I always got what I wanted.

Scarlett wasn't letting that happen.

For someone who had given up so much control in that private room, she certainly held on to it everywhere else.

I'd get to her, and I'd get her to listen.

Because, personally, I wasn't done tasting that woman. I wanted so much more of her in my mouth. And the farther she ran, the faster I wanted to chase her.

I was going to.

I just needed to try it a different way.

SEVEN

SCARLETT

THIS WAS my first day back at work since I'd returned from LA, and for the fifteen minutes I'd been at my desk, I couldn't take my eyes off my phone. More specifically, the last set of texts that I'd exchanged with Hudson the morning after Lush.

He must have thought I was an idiot.

Because an idiot would stay in the same hotel and not immediately check out.

Only an idiot would think it was a coincidence that we were both at the club that night and that he didn't have eyes all over me, tracking my every move.

I'd needed space. Privacy. And I'd needed to lose the tail.

So, I'd rented a house on the other side of the city, and that was where I'd spent the rest of my stay, holed up in a cute villa where I immersed myself in work and several bottles of wine.

Once I'd calmed down, I'd called Pepper. Initially, she hadn't wanted to tell me anything, as it was betraying client confidentiality. But, after I'd explained everything to her, she'd informed me that Hudson's membership was paid in full the night I saw him at Lush. To gain access so quickly, he had bypassed the typical registration period, and his approval had been expedited. There was a two-year waiting list, so it was unclear how this had happened.

Hudson knew someone. That was the only explanation.

Pepper just wasn't sure who that someone was.

She'd assured me she would talk to her employees and get to the bottom of it.

But it didn't matter at this point.

Hudson had already seen me naked.

He'd dominated my body.

He'd eaten my pussy.

Our professional relationship was severed with no chance of being repaired.

That wasn't to say I hadn't dated someone who worked with The Agency. Vince was a client of Jack's and had been the whole time we were together. But I didn't work directly with Vince, and I certainly wouldn't have slept with him to get him under contract.

What Hudson had done was premeditated.

He'd wanted to soften me, get me to a place where I'd agree to anything.

Fuck his way into closing this deal.

I despised him for it.

Part of me was mortified enough that I wanted to cancel the whole partnership. Walk away. Pretend as though Jayson, Shane, and Blake had never emailed me.

The other part of me wanted to bury Hudson, to use this experience as fuel and make him pay for his mistake.

Either way, I had to be careful. This wasn't just about me.

This was about the four of us, what the partnership could do for our business, our clients, and our future.

I couldn't let Hudson ruin that.

I'd given him control for one evening. Now, it was mine, and he wasn't getting it back.

I lifted my cell phone off my desk and carried it down the hall into Brett's office. Jack and Max were already in there, and the three of them were waiting for me.

"Good morning," I said.

"Morning," Jack and Max replied.

Brett nodded toward his desk where there was a Styrofoam cup sitting on the end of it. "I grabbed you a coffee."

I stepped through the doorway, took the coffee into my hand, and sat between Jack's and Max's chairs.

I hadn't seen my boys in several days. It had been even longer since I hung out with Max now that he was living in LA.

The three of them looked tired. Being on the road caused that, and lately, that was where they'd been spending most of their time.

But, after this past trip, I imagined I looked much worse than them.

"I hope you have some good news for us," Brett said.

I took a sip of the coffee and set it down, and my eyes connected with Brett's.

I'd weighed the different options during my walk to his office, and I kept reminding myself that what had happened with Hudson shouldn't affect them.

I had to take my personal life out of this equation.

I had to make this deal work.

Since we were kids, the guys had always told me everything. Even their deepest, darkest secrets. I knew all about the women they'd slept with, the ones who had turned into something more. I had seen the rings before they landed on any of the girls' fingers.

We'd been friends for almost my entire life.

They were my family.

And, when it came to me, they were extremely protective.

So, I had to lie and say, "We're close."

"How close?" Jack asked.

Because of the deadline I'd given our attorney, I said, "Less than a week."

Since I'd sent him that email from LA, telling him not to call unless the contract was ready to be signed, I hadn't heard from him.

That made me a little nervous.

"What happened in LA?" Brett asked. "You've told us nothing about your meeting with Hudson Jones."

The guys didn't know that I was a member of Lush. It wasn't something I was comfortable discussing with them. Even though I heard all about their sex lives, I never talked about mine. Therefore, I couldn't go into detail.

"There isn't anything to tell."

Brett looked at Jack and Max, and then I felt all their eyes on me.

They knew me too well.

Besides, I was a horrible liar.

They knew that, too.

"What we discussed isn't important," I clarified. "What matters is that we're at the end of the negotiations, and we should have a decision soon. Isn't that what we all want?"

Silence filled the room.

And then, several seconds later, Brett finally responded with, "Sure."

I had to get out of here before they started asking questions.

"I'll be chatting with our attorney today," I lied. "I'll let you know if he says anything important."

As I shifted in my seat, Jack said, "I thought you were communicating directly with Hudson now?"

Brett must have told him that, which was fine. It just made me realize how messy this was becoming.

"I am," I answered, feeling the heat start to spread across my face. "But, now that we're at the end, I think it's better that the communication stays between both attorneys. That way, everything is documented."

Max's eyes bore through me when he said, "Right."

It was time to get up and leave and get my mind off Hudson.

If we continued talking about him, they'd know something had happened between us. They'd be able to see it all over me, if they couldn't already.

Just as I went to stand, my phone vibrated in my hand. I felt my face redden even more as I read the text on the screen.

Hudson: We need to talk.

"Scarlett?" Brett said.

Hudson: I'm calling you in five minutes. Answer your phone.

"Scarlett?" Brett repeated.

I finally looked up from my cell, annoyed with myself that I hadn't blocked Hudson's number. "Yeah?"

"Do you want to talk about it?" Brett asked.

He knew something was bothering me.

As I glanced around at the other faces, I saw that they knew, too.

Damn it.

I held the phone against my chest, so they couldn't see the screen. "I have to make a call. I'll catch up with you guys in a little bit."

I walked out of his office and went straight into mine, locking the door behind me, giving no one a chance to barge in. Then, I set the phone on my desk and stared at it.

I wondered what he needed to talk to me about after I'd made it clear that I wanted nothing to do with him, that he needed to delete my number off his phone.

I should have known Hudson Jones wasn't the type of man who listened.

As my cell vibrated, indicating a call was coming through, his name appeared on the screen.

Maybe the guys were able to see right through me, but Hudson didn't have that advantage, and he wasn't here to read my face.

If he thought he was going to break me, he was about to get one hell of a surprise.

EIGHT
HUDSON

"HUDSON," Scarlett said as she answered my call. "I thought I'd made myself clear."

I placed my razor on the counter and wiped the rest of the shaving cream off my face, smiling from the sound of her angry voice.

I'd been craving her for the last few days.

Her begging.

Her body.

Her pussy that I hadn't been able to get enough of.

Her presence.

I liked being around that girl a little too much.

"We need to discuss the partnership," I said.

"No, we don't. If there's something that needs to be worked out, you can go through my attorney, like I told you before. But there shouldn't be anything that needs to be worked out. We're not budging. If your clients want to close, then they'll sign the paperwork. If not, we're prepared to walk."

"There's no reason for me to discuss anything with your attorney. This is between us."

When she laughed, I pictured her face. The way her neck tilted back to expose her throat. The way her lips spread over her perfect teeth. How the carefree noise warmed the color of her skin.

"You have no boundaries," she said. "I don't trust you. Not to mention, at this point, you've crossed so many lines, I'm not sure you're capable of seeing the real picture, so let me paint it for you, Mr. Jones—"

"Mmm," I growled when she said my name.

I wanted to hear her say it when I had a fucking clamp around her nipple, and I was flicking the end of it with my finger.

"Did you just moan?" she snapped.

"I love it when you're pissed."

"I'm going to hang up."

She could be as strong as she wanted, but I could still tell that I affected her.

"No, you're not," I said, tightening the towel around my waist as I went into my closet.

Since I'd be traveling today, I grabbed a pair of jeans and a button-down and brought them over to my bed. I pressed the Speaker button, so I could get dressed at the same time.

"You'll want to listen to what I have to say because whatever is in that head of yours is all wrong, I promise you."

"Hudson, let me give you a tip. If you want me to do something, don't start by telling me I'm wrong. That will never go over well."

"Then, how about I tell you how good your pussy tasted?"

"Now, I'm really hanging up."

I'd found her weakness.

It was sex.

"And how hard you groaned when you came on my tongue." I paused, waiting for her to respond. There was only silence. "And the look on your face when you asked for my cock."

"Good-bye, Hud—"

"Something tells me you've been thinking about me as much as I've been thinking about you."

She said nothing.

"Why don't you stop threatening to hang up, so I can break it all down for you, and we can end this bullshit?"

I had her.

And it felt so fucking good.

"Let me tell you something, Hudson." Her voice turned even sharper, and it made my dick hard. "I'm not on a bed right now, tied by my wrists and ankles. The days of me being submissive to you are long over. So, instead of saying *cherry*, I'm going to do this..."

There was a click.

And then the phone went dead.

I finished buttoning the shirt and lifted my cell off the bed, sliding it into my back pocket.

She could hang up all she wanted.

But she couldn't hide.

NINE

SCARLETT

"WHAT A DICK," I said as I hung up on Hudson and dropped the phone on my desk.

That man really had some nerve to tell me I was wrong, that I needed to listen, and then start demanding things from me. He'd lost that privilege the second he manipulated me into believing his name was Andrew and brought me into the private room to blackmail me.

If he explained his reasoning, it would only cause me to hate him more.

The thing that pissed me off the most was that Hudson was extremely attractive, he had the most talented tongue, and his hands knew how to hurt me just right. While I'd stood with him at the bar at Lush, I'd considered coming back the following evening just to see him again.

He was that good.

That attentive.

That enticing.

Now, the thought of him made my skin crawl.

I sighed, ignoring the screen of my phone as it lit up with different messages, and I turned toward my computer. I wasn't even through the first email when there was a knock at my door.

"Yes?" I called out.

The handle jiggled. Whoever it was, was trying to get in and couldn't with the door locked.

"It's Brett," the knocker said.

He would have called from his office if he wanted something quick.

Therefore, I knew this was going to be a long conversation.

I walked over to the door and unlocked it, so he could come in.

He shut it behind him and followed me over to my desk where he took a seat in front of me. "You know why I'm here."

I appreciated him getting straight to the point. There was nothing worse than small talk when there was a motive behind it.

I crossed my arms over my chest. "Were you elected, or did you draw straws?"

His grin was small but warm. "We didn't think you'd like all three of us coming in here to question you."

"You thought correctly."

Brett certainly wasn't the softest of the three guys. That would be Jack. But I understood why Brett had been chosen. He had a way with words, and he was the smoothest. And, even though I was very close to Max and Jack, Brett and I always had a little stronger connection.

"What the hell is going on with you, Scarlett?"

My thumb pressed against the side of my mouth, and I

chewed the skin around my nail. "My meeting with Hudson didn't go the way I'd intended."

His brows rose. "Explain."

I couldn't be honest with him. There was just no way. If I were, I feared all three of my boys would be on our plane, heading for LA, and it wouldn't be pretty. What Hudson had done was wrong on so many levels, but ratting him out wasn't my style.

This was my problem, not theirs.

"Things didn't exactly stay professional," I told him.

His leg crossed, his shoe resting on his other thigh. "Is this going to fuck up the deal?"

I'd been asking myself the same question since I left Lush.

"Brett, I honestly don't know."

I watched him process what I'd just said.

"How did you leave things with him?"

I shook my head. "Not in a good way."

I could tell there were more questions he wanted to ask. Before he went there, I needed to redirect. The last person I wanted to protect was Hudson, but I feared Brett was taking my side, and I didn't want there to be animosity if we were all in a conference room together.

It would be better if the guys blamed me than Hudson.

I was forgivable.

He wasn't.

"Brett, this is my fault, and I take full responsibility. It was a bad judgment call, and it shouldn't have happened. I promise I'm going to do everything I can to make sure things go through the way we want them to and that my situation with Hudson won't affect the partnership deal."

As he stared at me, I knew he was analyzing every word that had come out of my mouth.

It took him a while before he finally said, "This isn't like you."

He was right.

It hadn't been like me to hook up with the attorney representing the other side. And, had I known who he was, I wouldn't have let him touch me.

But Brett wasn't getting the real story.

"Listen, I'm fine, so before you start asking if I want to talk about it, you don't have to."

His gaze intensified. "You sure about that?"

I hated that he could see right through me.

And I hated that I was going to hell for lying to my best friend.

"Stop worrying about me," I told him.

Instead of giving me another smile, he nodded, and then he stood and moved over to the door.

Even though he'd been fairly easy on me, I was relieved that the interrogation was over.

Just as I glanced at my computer screen to return to my email, I heard, "Scarlett?"

I turned toward the doorway where he stood. "Yes?"

"When you're ready to tell me the truth, I'll be here, waiting."

That fucker.

"Get back to work," I ordered, rolling my eyes at him since we both knew I'd been busted. "And shut my door."

Once it was closed, my elbows landed on the desk, my hands pressing against the sides of my head so that I could rub my temples.

Brett wouldn't push.

None of the guys would.

But knowing they were onto me was going to make this even harder.

Until this deal was either agreed upon or squashed, I was going to have lots of eyes on me.

More than I was comfortable with.

I didn't leave the office until some time after nine. As usual, I was the last one there. Most of the employees were gone by six. And the guys had checked out around seven to go to dinner together since Max was in town.

I'd decided to skip.

Partly because I didn't want to face them all tonight.

And partly because I had so much work to do, and a few uninterrupted hours would allow me to get some of it done.

Since I lived in a high-rise only three blocks from the office, I almost always walked home instead of using the company's driver, and I was doing the same tonight.

It was a hot evening, so I draped my suit jacket over my forearm and slung my bag over my shoulder, and I went out through the front lobby. As I headed toward the first crosswalk, I recapped the whole day in my head.

At least, the highlights.

More like the conversation I'd had with Brett and how I still hadn't heard from our attorney. The partnership was at a complete standstill, and I worried that the only way to change that was by speaking to Hudson.

I had a feeling today wasn't going to be the last time he

reached out, but until this deal went through, I didn't want to block him on my phone.

I just couldn't imagine what I would say to him.

He was relentless when it came to discussing the night at Lush. And that was a topic I really wanted to avoid. *So, how the hell can I get us moving in the right direction when he's so stuck on that evening?*

I was waiting for that answer to come to me as I walked the last block to my building.

Even at this hour, the streets were so loud and extremely busy. I couldn't wait to get upstairs to my penthouse and pour myself a glass of wine, change into something comfortable, and shut out the sounds of the city. Maybe I would even take a bath, so I could soak the day off.

As I approached the front entrance, the doorman came outside and opened the door for me. I was a few steps away from entering when I heard my name being spoken from somewhere behind me.

My feet stopped moving.

My hands began to shake.

It was that voice.

The one I'd heard at Lush.

The one I hadn't recognized at the time because, the few instances we'd spoken on the phone, he had sounded nasally and sick.

I took a deep breath, and I slowly glanced over my shoulder.

Hudson was standing less than ten feet away.

He looked different than the last time I'd seen him. He was casual—not as put together, but just as handsome. Possibly even more so, which I hated.

I didn't like the feeling that was in my chest.

I didn't like that there was a buzz inside my body as I glanced at his hands.

I didn't like that my reaction to him wasn't just physical.

I didn't like that he had any effect on me at all.

I cleared my throat, gritted my teeth together, and said, "What in the hell are you doing here?"

TEN
HUDSON

I WALKED down the sidewalk and stopped when my body was only a few inches from Scarlett's. I expected her to immediately push me away, but she stood still with a stunned expression on her face.

"We need to talk," I told her.

The shock finally left her, and she took several steps back, putting distance between us. "You came all the way across the country to tell me that?"

"You hung up on me. You gave me no other choice."

"That's because I have nothing to say to you, and I still don't. So, go back to where you came from, Hudson—"

"You need to let me explain myself."

She shook her head. "Nope, not interested."

She turned back toward the door. When she took a step, I grabbed her wrist and stopped her from moving.

"Just hear me out, Scarlett. Ten minutes of your time. Once I'm done, you can kick me out."

"Miss Davis," the doorman said, "if this man is bothering you, I'll call the police."

"Everything is fine," she told him. Then, she glanced over her shoulder and glared at me. "You think I'm going to let you inside my condo?"

"Yes."

"You're fucking crazy."

She should have been an attorney. She was more ruthless than half of the fucking lawyers at my firm.

"Scarlett, I came almost three thousand miles to have a conversation with you. All I'm asking is that you give me a chance to explain myself. You don't have to forgive me or stop hating me; you just have to give me your attention for a short period of time."

She said nothing; she also hadn't pulled her hand out of my grasp.

"If you're more comfortable with talking down here, that's fine, but I don't think you want anyone hearing those kinds of details." I could tell she was thinking about it and was on the verge of responding, so I added, "I'll leave right after. You have my word."

"Your word means shit."

I threw my hand in the air. "Then, have security wait outside the door if that makes you feel better."

Her eyes squinted as she studied me. "Ten minutes."

I nodded. "That's all I want."

I released her wrist and followed her inside to the elevator. Once it opened, we walked in, and she waved a fob over a small black reader before she hit the PH button.

The penthouse.

I'd expected nothing less from Scarlett Davis.

She didn't say a word the entire ride and kept her focus on the door.

Mine was on her.

God, she looked fucking gorgeous tonight. She was dressed in a suit and had taken the jacket off, hanging it over her arm. The shirt hugged the curves of her body and the roundness of her tits. The pants were fitted, and that heart-shaped ass was taunting me.

If she hadn't looked at me so seriously and with so much disgust, I would have hit the Stop button on the elevator, held her against the wall, and fucked her until she screamed.

But that wasn't even an option.

Still, it felt good as hell to just be around her again.

When the door opened, I saw that we were directly inside her condo. She led me through a foyer and a massive open space that was several rooms combined into one. It was impressive as hell. So were the wall of windows that overlooked downtown, a sight that hit you the second you walked into the room.

Scarlett went straight to the kitchen and grabbed a wine glass from the cabinet, pouring herself some red from a bottle on the counter. She held the glass close while she watched me from the other side of the island where I was waiting for her to look at me.

"I'd offer you some, but you won't be staying long enough to drink it."

"Fair enough."

"You have my attention, so talk."

Her eyes were still on me. In fact, I was sure they were boring a goddamn hole right through me.

I cleared my throat and pressed my hands on the stone.

"The reason I wanted you in LA was because I thought we could get more accomplished in person than going back and forth on the phone and through email. And, since there was a good chance you wouldn't want to see me outside the office, my plan was to show up wherever you were that night."

"What if I hadn't gone out?"

I shrugged. "I'd have seen you at the hotel bar."

"And if I hadn't left my room?"

"I would have knocked on your door."

By the look on her face, I could tell that answer didn't make her happy.

But I was here to speak the truth, and that was what I was giving her.

She wrapped an arm around her stomach and said, "I don't understand something. If what you wanted to discuss was work-related, then why meet outside your office?"

"From my experience, when you're working on a deal as large as this one, it can help."

She stared at me like I had a fucking monkey on my head. "You mean to tell me, you track down the party you're not representing, and you meet with them without their attorney present and bully them into signing the contract?"

"Not all cases, just some."

Her lip curled. "Oh my God."

"And I wouldn't call it bullying. All I do is lay out the terms, so they understand them better, and I give them a gentle push."

"I don't believe you."

"I'm not lying, Scarlett. Despite what you think, you can trust me."

Her expression toned down a little, but it was still so hard and edgy. "Don't use a word you don't know the meaning of."

I shook my goddamn head. "Listen to me; never did it cross my mind that you wouldn't know who I was. I thought, the second I came up behind you at Lush, you'd turn around and start yelling at me, demanding to know why I was there."

She took a drink of her wine. "How would I have known it was you? We'd never met before."

"I figured you'd Googled me."

"Why would I care what you looked like?"

"Had you cared, we wouldn't be in this situation."

She set her wine glass down, flattened her hands on the countertop, and slowly looked up at me. "I can't believe what I'm hearing right now." She paused. "You're actually blaming me for not Googling you when the reason this all happened is because you were dishonest and told me your name was Andrew."

"Andrew is my middle name."

"That's still a lie. Had you said Hudson Jones, I would have known who you were. But you didn't because you liked that I was in the dark. You liked that you got a piece of me."

"Why does it matter if you didn't know who I was? That's the whole point of Lush, isn't it? To find someone you're attracted to and experience things in a safe environment. I would imagine you don't know most of the people you're intimate with there."

"Except I didn't want to be touched by the attorney who's representing the other side of this business deal. I wanted to get touched by someone I had no personal connection to."

"Stranger or not, do you really think that's possible in LA?"

She sighed. "I'm having a conversation with a man who's incapable of admitting he did anything wrong."

"The conversation we're having is to get you to understand that I didn't lead you into the private room to get something I would later hold against you. I took you in there because I wanted my hands on you. I wanted to inflict pain and pleasure. I wanted to dominate the fuck out of you." She didn't stop me, so I continued, "As soon as I realized you didn't know who I was, it was no longer about business. That shit became personal. Real fast."

Her gaze didn't move, nor did it soften.

"I instantly forgot who I was representing, and it was all about you."

"That doesn't change the fact that you lied to me."

She was fixated on the wrong thing, but if this was what she needed, then I'd give it to her.

"Yes, Scarlett, I lied to you about my name. I should have been honest about it from the beginning. But that would have meant I couldn't touch you. I didn't want you to take that away from me."

"But you took that choice away from me."

"I did," I admitted. "And it was wrong of me."

Her hand returned to the stem of her wine glass, her posture relaxing a little. "I don't want you discussing what happened at Lush with anyone. Do you understand me?"

"You have nothing to worry about."

"Good." She took another drink of her red. "Then, I think we're done here."

There was nothing left to say about that night. Anything else would just be a repeat at this point.

"Are you ready to move on from this?" I asked her.

She didn't answer for several seconds. Then, she backed up until her ass hit the sink, and she leaned into the edge of it. "I'm not sure why this is even relevant, but yes, we can move on. However, that changes nothing. The communication will still be between you and my attorney."

"I see."

"Hudson, we were strangers before this, and we'll be strangers after."

I hadn't expected her to say anything different, but I was still disappointed.

I wanted her tied up.

I wanted my fucking hands on her.

They twitched on top of the stone now that we were this close again.

And I wanted to spend time with her when she wasn't naked and roped, when I could get some of her beautiful laughter and that smile I couldn't get enough of. She'd given me a taste of her personality, her wit and charm.

I wanted more.

"I think it's time for you to go," she said before I responded.

She moved from her side of the counter toward the foyer, and she pressed the button when she reached the elevator.

I followed her, and when the elevator opened, I stopped right in front of her. She didn't push me away, so I bent down and put my face in her neck. I saw her take in a breath and hold it, her chest rising and falling much faster than it needed to.

I still affected her.

So, I went in deeper, and once I felt her skin, I inhaled, taking in her amber scent. It was the sexiest fucking smell.

Then, I grazed my nose against the side of her neck, slowing as I reached the bottom of her ear. My lips pressed against it just briefly as I said, "Good-bye, Scarlett."

She said nothing as I stepped inside the elevator or when I turned around to stare at her gorgeous face. She still didn't say a word when the door closed.

When I got into the lobby, I phoned the driver, and he picked me up in front of her building. I waited until I was in the backseat before I opened my email.

I'd already been given the authorization from Jayson, Shane, and Blake to proceed with the partnership. They were done negotiating. So, I sent the email I had drafted on the plane to The Agency's attorney, letting him know my clients accepted the final terms. Once the email went through, I clicked on the last text I'd sent to Scarlett, and I began to type.

Me: You'll be hearing from your attorney in the morning. Congratulations. You just got the deal of a lifetime.

ELEVEN
SCARLETT

AS WE APPROACHED the South Beach location of Lush, the driver looked at me in the rearview mirror and said, "Do you want me to wait for you in the parking lot across the street?"

"Yes," I answered.

My eyes then lowered to the screen of my phone. Almost the entire time I'd been in this backseat, I'd been staring at the text Hudson had sent almost an hour ago.

The deal was done.

Entertainment Management Worldwide was now going to be a part of The Agency.

After all that hard work, negotiation, the stress over whether the merger was going to go through or not, we'd gotten the percentage we'd asked for.

So, even though I'd planned on staying in tonight, taking a bath and soaking the day off, I'd decided to put on a tight, strapless black dress and go out to celebrate.

I had Hudson to thank for that.

All I'd had to do was play nice, let him inside my condo, and listen to what he had to say, and then I'd gotten everything I wanted.

It hadn't come easy.

The man was an expert with words.

Now, I understood why he was an excellent attorney and one of the most successful in LA. It was almost impossible to get him to admit he'd done anything wrong. But, once he'd finally given in, I'd rushed him out of my house. I'd needed to get away from him. Our chemistry was too strong, and I didn't trust myself around him.

Not when my body silently screamed for his touch.

I should have figured he wouldn't just get in the elevator and go downstairs. He'd had to caress me one last time. And, tonight, he had used his lips.

It was a good thing the elevator door closed when it did.

I would only be seeing Hudson one more time. That would be when the boys and I flew out to LA to sign the paperwork for the partnership and to meet with Jayson, Blake, and Shane. Then, things between us would return to the way they had been before—nonexistent.

I didn't know what would happen if I decided to move back to California and run the finance division for our office there. That thought had been running through my mind since I returned from my last trip. God, I missed LA. But, now that Hudson had a membership, one I didn't know if Pepper would revoke when she was finished with her investigation, there was a chance I could run into him at the West Coast club.

I wasn't sure how I felt about that.

Or how I felt about the flutters inside my chest every time I thought of him.

I just knew, when his smell hit my nose and his sounds filled my ears, I became vulnerable.

I wanted to be dominated.

I wanted to lose control.

I didn't know if I could stop myself from being with him.

And I didn't know if I could stop myself from begging for it.

One command from Hudson Jones, and I'd be kneeling.

My pussy started to tingle.

To calm it down, I dragged my eyes away from Hudson's text and slipped my phone into the pocket behind the driver's seat.

The driver parked along the curb in front of the entrance and said, "Have the receptionist call me when you're ready to leave, and I'll pick you up." He came around to the backseat and helped me out.

I released his hand and walked up to the door where I knocked twice. The security guard opened it and held a tablet in my direction. I set my hand on the middle of the screen.

When there was a green glow underneath my fingers, he said, "Welcome, Miss Davis."

"Thank you."

I stepped inside and was greeted by the women in the reception area. I smiled at them and moved straight to the locked door. I only stood there for a few seconds before it slowly started to open.

As soon as the space was large enough for me to fit through, the scent of sex instantly hit me.

I closed my eyes for just a second and inhaled the deliciousness.

The feeling that had burst through my clit moments ago in the SUV was back.

It reinforced one thing.

Lush was exactly where I wanted to celebrate tonight.

As I headed toward the back, I noticed how similar this club was to the one in LA. The layout was identical. So were the colors and textures. The furniture was slightly different, and the decorations varied. Miami was a little more sleek and contemporary, and it was extremely glitzy. It felt much more like South Florida in here. LA's club had more of a traditional and ornate theme, and it seemed overly rich and luxurious in there.

Just like I had done at the other location, I avoided the center of the room where people were gathered and quietly talking at the tables and couches, and I went to the bar. I ordered some champagne, and once the bartender handed me a glass, I wandered down one of the hallways. One that I knew had six rooms that were completely open for viewing.

I just wanted to watch a fantasy.

I wanted to watch how it was played out.

I wanted skin.

I wanted sounds and smells and movements of the body that made my clit throb even harder.

I found one almost immediately.

There was a woman, completely naked, shackled to an armless wooden chair. Handcuffs were around her wrists and ankles. The man standing behind her held a feather crop. He was circling it around her breasts and going back and forth across her nipples. There was a second man in the room. He was kneeling in front of her, his fingers gripping a leather strap that he was smacking against her pussy.

74

She begged for the leather.

It slapped her.

She asked him to hit her harder.

The sound got louder as he complied.

Each time the belt landed on her skin, I would jump.

And, each time, the surge between my legs would grow, and I'd squeeze them together even tighter. The sensation was spreading to my nipples and into my chest and up my throat.

My neck tilted back, my mouth opened, and my eyes closed.

And, just as a soft, pent-up moan started to fall from my lips, I felt something behind me.

Based on the height, I knew it was a man.

I felt his hard, tight chest as it pressed against my bare shoulders. The clenching of his hands as they cinched my waist. The scent of his aftershave as his mouth came close to my neck.

I held my breath.

As I recognized his smell that was now filling my nose, my entire body began to hum.

"You need pain," he growled.

I need pain.

"You need the release."

I need the release.

"You need the excitement."

I need the excitement.

"You need the sting."

I need the sting.

My lips had closed the second I smelled him, but they opened again and exhaled, "Yes."

"You want me to tie you up and give it all to you."

Nothing he'd said was phrased as a question.

That wasn't his role.

Instead, he was giving me a warning. A chance to say no before he grabbed my hand and led me somewhere.

But that was what I wanted.

My submissive side had completely taken over.

I knew what he was capable of doing to my body.

It was what I needed.

Now.

So, I tilted my face and moaned, "Yes," into Hudson's ear.

TWELVE
HUDSON

EVERYTHING SCARLETT WORE MADE her look incredibly sexy.

But none of the outfits I'd seen her wear compared to the one I was dressing her in right now.

Rope.

That was all that was going to cover her skin.

I'd really taken my time with it, using the techniques I'd studied and perfected over the last eight years while I weaved the rough material across each wrist and around the middle of her arms. It then went over the top and bottom of her tits, her navel, and the center of her pussy. Several more strips went on her legs before the final wrap was secured around both ankles. Each piece was then tied to the back of the wooden Saint Andrew's Cross she was pressed up against in the private room I'd taken her into.

After I finished checking the last knot, I took several steps back to view the whole picture.

Scarlett's eyes were hungry, her lips wet and ready.

She was restrained and couldn't move more than an inch.

She was fully submissive.

And mine.

Fuck me.

"You're gorgeous," I hissed.

She was art.

She was my art.

And I didn't want to wait another second to paint her body with dominance.

I opened the dresser drawer, viewing all of my options. Riding crops, floggers, canes, paddles. I went with the flogger, and I stood right in front of her as I said, "Tell me your safe word."

"Cherry." Even her voice was thick with need.

It was so fucking hard not to touch her, not to dip my cock into her pussy, fucking her as hard as I could.

There would be time for that.

Right now, I was really going to enjoy this.

I raised my arm in the air and dropped it, using a fast diagonal motion.

The tips of the leather whipped across her nipple, and she cried out, "Yes. More, please."

That sound was so fucking hot.

With her tits squeezed between the ropes, the blood was draining to them, and each slash was turning them even redder.

It was also starting to feel more intense for her.

I could tell because she was becoming louder.

Her cries more guttural.

"Hudson!" she shouted after about the tenth one.

My dick was already so fucking hard. Now that I'd heard my name come out of her mouth, it felt like my hard-on was going to bust through my goddamn pants.

"That's it," I said after another slap. "Give me all your control."

When the leather moved across her body, I wasn't just listening to her sounds. I was watching her eyes and the way her nostrils flared when she quickly sucked in air. I was observing the jumping of her body, the contraction of her muscles, the way she squirmed against the rope.

I was waiting for *cherry*.

I wasn't aiming for it.

I was just prepared to hear it.

But she never said it.

Her adrenaline had taken over. With each hit, more of it built, causing her pain threshold to rise. Her body was releasing endorphins from the constant stimulation. And, although I'd switched to a mild pressure and I'd increased the amount of time between each whip, I could feel a high coming over her.

That meant she could handle more pain.

That her body didn't wiggle as much.

That she was slipping further into an endorphin high.

With her neck being the only part of her that wasn't bound to the cross, she lifted her chin and ground the back of her head into the wood. Pleasure spread across her lips. Her eyes started to close, and she moaned, "Hudson," dragging out each syllable.

I loved that sound.

And, because I was so close to her, I could almost feel the vibration of her tongue.

Jesus fucking Christ.

I was holding the flogger in the air and counting down to twenty before I lowered it. When I reached eleven, Scarlett's eyes opened.

Her face had the same expression as when she'd gotten off from my tongue—satisfaction in her eyes, teeth gnawing her lower lip, skin extremely red and damp.

She'd reached that headspace, and now, she was climbing her way down.

"How do you feel?" I asked.

As I waited for her to answer, I checked out her skin. The tails of the flogger had done a good amount of damage. She didn't have any open wounds, but blood had risen to the top of her flesh, and some of her marks were going to take days to heal.

Having her go into full-blown sub-space would take her far too long to recover from. And, if I continued using the flogger, that was what would happen. So, I let it fall from my hand, and I moved behind the cross, loosening each of the knots until she could slip her body out.

I joined her and wrapped my hand around hers. I led her toward the chair in the corner of the room and sat her down. There was a blanket on the back, which I opened up and wrapped over her shoulders.

"Are you all right?" I asked.

She was so vulnerable in this moment, and taking care of her felt so fucking good.

Since she was shivering a little, telling me her temperature had dropped, I gently rubbed my hands over her arms and down her legs. Then, I knelt at her feet and pulled one into my palms, massaging the top and her toes and heel.

"I'm okay," she said softly.

"There's medicine I can rub on your welts." I pointed at the dresser where I'd found several bottles of lotion and antibacterial gel. "It might make them feel better."

"I'm fine," she said. "I don't need anything." Her lips eventually stopped quivering, and she moved the blanket off her neck. The foot I wasn't working on was now pressing against my thigh, her toes inching closer to my cock. "I want to suck your dick. Please put it in my mouth."

"Scarlett, I was just so rough on your body. You don't have to do this."

"I want to. Not just for you, but for me, too."

She waited for me to get to my feet before she pushed herself off the chair and got on her knees. She undid my belt buckle and then my button and zipper, finally pulling my cock out of my boxer briefs. Since I was so fucking hard, it came out of my pants like a goddamn spring.

"*Mmm*," Scarlett groaned as she aligned her mouth with my tip. "God, your dick is beautiful."

Her lips parted, and she surrounded my crown, sucking it hard, swirling her tongue around it.

"Shit," I roared. The feeling of her was just too fucking good.

Her hand circled the base of me and pumped to the middle and back down, dragging some of the spit that had fallen from her mouth.

"Take it nice and deep," I growled.

I could stare at this fucking sight forever.

Scarlett's eyelids were wide and a little watery from the way I was thrusting inside her mouth. Her cheeks were drawn in as she sucked. Both hands were now wrapped around my shaft. The amount of spit covering me reminded me of how wet her pussy had gotten the night I ate it.

As incredible as this felt, I wanted her cunt.

I reached down and lifted her off the floor.

"More," she demanded. There was still so much need in her voice. "Please."

I carried her to the bed and set her on the end of it. "You'll get what I give you."

I went to the nightstand and grabbed a condom from the top drawer. As I moved back over to her, I started shedding the clothes from my body. Once I was naked, I opened the foil and slid the condom on. I stepped to the foot of the bed.

"Get on your knees, beautiful," I ordered.

She rose from a seated position and knelt in front of me.

"Turn around and give me that sexy ass," I said.

She twisted in a semicircle, her ass now pointed in my direction.

Damn it, it was a good one.

Not too thin or flat, just the right amount to grab.

I brought my hand back and slapped the right side of it, my fingers lifting just before I reached her hip.

"Yes," she yelped, and it was one of the sexiest sounds I'd ever heard. "Again, please."

I spanked her with even more power this time, covering almost half of her ass.

"Yes!" she screamed. "Harder, please."

When my hand went back down, it wasn't to hit her. It was

to grip the outside of her thighs. Then, I reared my hips back, and I plunged my cock straight into her cunt.

"Hudson," she moaned.

I moaned louder than her.

Because nothing, not even when my tongue was on her, could have prepared me for the tightness I felt inside her pussy.

The wetness.

The heat.

It felt like she was squeezing my cock.

As I worked my way in, I rotated my hips in a circle, feeling the different spots within her that I was able to hit, and then I pulled back to the tip. That was a pattern I continued, sliding into the base of my shaft and going out to my crown.

Since my fingers knew what she felt like when she came from the last time we had been here, I could tell she was getting close.

So, I slid all the way out. I reached underneath her and flipped her onto her back.

I wanted her eyes on me when her pussy milked my cum.

I parted her legs and put one over each of my shoulders. Holding her by the hips, I steered her cunt to my cock. And, once I found the entrance, it felt like she practically sucked me back in.

"Fuck," I hissed as her wetness swallowed me.

My cock thrust in and out, finding the rhythm I'd had before, rotating in a circle when I was fully plunged. Within a few strokes, the tingling set in, moving through my balls. Knowing this would take her over the edge, I put my thumb on her clit and rubbed it back and forth.

"Oh God," she cried. "Yes!"

MARNI MANN

The feeling was working its way into my stomach, and there was a moment when everything inside me tightened, the build reaching a peak before I shot my first load.

"Scarlett," I breathed.

Her eyes caught mine while my cock gave her hard, deep thrusts to work out the rest of my orgasm.

"Yes," she moaned. "I am, too."

She didn't have to tell me she was coming.

I felt each time her pussy contracted. And I saw each wave of pleasure that spread through her body because it caused her navel to shudder.

I slowed down my movements as I pumped out the rest of my load and finally pulled out. "Fuck, that was good," I said, sliding her legs off my shoulders and setting her thighs on the bed.

She leaned up and moved to the very edge, her hands going to my stomach. She ran them to my chest, around my pecs, and back down to my abs.

"Your body," she said, looking up at my eyes. "It's more perfect than I thought it would be."

I'd felt the same way about her.

Even more so now that my cock had been inside her, and I knew what she really felt like.

"Are you flying back tomorrow?"

I nodded.

"Do you need to go to bed early?" Her smile was sexy as hell and a little devious.

I knew exactly what she was thinking. "You want more."

Her teeth sank down into the corner of her lip. "Don't you?"

Just when her hand went to reach for my cock, I grabbed

84

her wrist and said, "Put your hands behind your back and push yourself to the top of the bed. When you get there, I want you clinging to the headboard. Don't you dare let go."

Her mouth opened, and her head leaned back as she moaned, "Yes, sir."

THIRTEEN

SCARLETT

Me: Headed back home?

Hudson: On the plane right now.

Me: Just wanted to let you know, I heard from our attorney. Looks like I'll be coming to LA in a week.

Hudson: I'm going to kidnap you and take you to dinner.

Me: As in a date?

Hudson: I can chain you to the chair and feed you myself if you'd like that better.

Me: Let's skip the food and go straight to the chains.

Hudson: You're opposed to eating.

Me: I'm opposed to going on a date.

Hudson: Because?

Me: You lied to me, Hudson. I haven't forgotten about that. For now, I want things to stay the way they are.

Hudson: You just want to fuck.

Me: Yes, and I want you to give me the best fucking I've ever had.

Hudson: You'll get what you want...for now.

I READ Hudson's texts over and over again and smiled.

Even though we'd spent most of last night together, we hadn't discussed anything during our time at Lush besides how good we were both feeling.

Our past was a topic we'd avoided completely.

Had we started hashing out our disagreement before he took me to the private room, things would have gotten heated. And then nothing would have happened between us.

But the second I'd walked into the club, only a few things had mattered.

The loss of control.

Submission.

And finding that release I needed.

Just because we'd fucked didn't mean I'd gotten over Hudson lying to me or that he'd told me to come to LA so that he could persuade me into settling.

That was just dirty.

That was also why I wanted to keep things right where they were.

I didn't trust him outside of Lush.

But I loved what he did to my body, the way he provided so much after-care. I loved the way he fucked me, the way that deliciously large cock could reach the end of me and find spots most men couldn't. And I loved how I felt safe even when he was hurting me, and how when it was time to leave I didn't want to go.

Me: I'm excited to find out what you have planned.
Hudson: Is your pussy sore today?
Me: A little.
Hudson: Can I be rougher next time?

Me: Yes.
Hudson: Then, plan on not being able to walk.
Me: Mmm. I like the sound of that.

I tucked my phone under my fingers and walked down the hall toward Brett's office. "Hey," I said as I got to the doorway.

He looked up from his computer and waved his hand in the air. "Come in."

As I was moving over to the chair in front of his desk, Jack came in behind me.

He sat next to me and said, "Morning, guys."

"Morning," I replied.

I reached for Brett's office phone. I turned it around to face me, and then I hit the preprogrammed button that would call Max's cell. Now that he was based in LA, this was how we conducted most of our meetings. Once it began to ring, I hit Speaker and leaned back in my chair.

"What's up, guys?" Max said as he answered.

"Hey, Max," I said. I waited for the other guys to respond before I continued, "I know we only have a few minutes to chat, so I'll be quick. I spoke to our attorney this morning, and Entertainment Management Worldwide has agreed to our terms. They're ready to close, and they want us to fly to LA in a week to sign the paperwork."

"Hell fucking yes," Jack said.

I felt Brett's eyes on me when he commented, "Fuck yeah. I was wondering if this was ever going to go through. I'm so fucking happy we got what we wanted."

"Great news, Scarlett," Max said. "I couldn't be more fucking pleased."

I was happy the guys were excited that we'd finally come to an agreement.

"I've checked all of your schedules," I told them. "The three of you are supposed to be on the road that day, so it's going to take some rearranging. You'll need to talk to your assistants and get them to start reworking your appointments."

"I'm all over it," Brett answered.

"Me, too," Max said.

"Man, once the papers are signed, there's going to be a hell of a lot of work to do," Jack said. "We have two LA offices we need to merge."

I looked at Jack and said, "Plus, a location in Manhattan that now needs to be staffed with agents."

"So, you're saying this is a bad time to tell you that I'm going to Italy for two weeks?" Max asked.

Everyone in this room laughed.

"You're not going anywhere," I told him. "At least, not until we figure out the logistics of this. Then, I'm sure I can come to LA and take over while you're gone."

"God, she's a hard-ass," Max said.

This time, I grinned and said, "The hard-ass is hanging up. Talk to you later, Max."

"Congratulations, you fuckers," Max said before Brett ended the call.

"It's finally happened," Jack said, standing from his seat, his expression telling me it had all suddenly kicked in. He moved to the doorway and held on to the frame while he looked back at us. "Lunch today to celebrate?"

"I think I can swing that," Brett said.

"Me, too," I agreed.

Jack left and shut the office door behind him.

As I started to get up, Brett said, "Sit."

I wasn't surprised by his command. I just didn't take orders well when I wasn't inside Lush. "I'm sitting."

"Will you tell me what you had to do to get this deal done?"

I thought about his question and considered it. And then I promptly decided against it. "One day, I'll tell you everything but not today."

He crossed his arms over his chest. "You used to tell me everything. When did that change?"

"Definitely not everything." My voice softened. "Like I never tell you about the men I date."

"Why don't you?"

I smiled and stood, this time making it all the way to my feet. "Because my stories would have to come with body armor."

"You're saying, I have an anger problem?"

None of the guys did.

But we were from Boston.

We had pride.

We believed in taking care of what was ours.

And, where we were from, the bond between friends was as thick as family.

"I'm saying, you're protective; that's all."

As I walked to the door, he said, "Scarlett." When I looked over my shoulder, he added, "I'm still worried about you."

"Don't be. I'm fine."

"You said that last time."

He was right.

I smiled, and it felt so good. "But, this time, I really mean it."

FOURTEEN
HUDSON

Me: *Three days.*
Scarlett: *Is your hand starting to twitch for my ass?*
Me: *Not just my hand.*
Scarlett: *I think your cock misses me.*
Me: *I think you miss it just as much.*

Me: *Two.*
Scarlett: *You're not counting or anything.*
Me: *You can tell me you don't like it, but I know that would be a lie.*
Scarlett: *I don't lie, Mr. Jones.*
Me: *I know what you're implying, and I'm going to punish you for that.*
Scarlett: *I was hoping you'd say that.*

> Me: *Are you on the plane?*
> Scarlett: *We just landed.*
> Me: *It's going to be so fucking hard not to touch you in my office.*
> Scarlett: *Who said you couldn't?*
> Me: *Dirty, dirty girl.*

"MR. JONES," Tina said through the speaker of my office line, "the gentlemen from Entertainment Management World-wide have just arrived, and I've brought them into your conference room. The Agency and their attorney are also here, but I've sat them in the lobby. Would you like me to bring them in as well?"

I checked the time on my computer screen and did some quick math in my head. Then, I said, "Bring them into the conference room in twelve minutes. Not a second later."

"No problem."

I hung up and got up from my desk, heading one floor down to where my conference room was located. We had several in our building, but I had my own—perks of being one of the founding partners.

I gave the door a quick knock before I opened it and went in. My clients—Jayson, Shane, and Blake—were sitting at the far end of the table. The room turned silent as they all looked in my direction. When they saw it was me, the three of them stood.

"Good morning, fellas," I said as I made my way over to them.

"Morning," they each responded separately as they shook my hand.

I took a seat at the head of the table, resting my ass on the very edge of the chair. "In a few minutes, my assistant is going to bring in the partners of The Agency and their attorney. Everything is pretty straightforward at this point. We're going to present the contract, which all of you have already read several times, and we're going to ask for a series of signatures. The funds are already in escrow, so we'll discuss the logistics and the next steps, and then you're free to go. Once those signatures are inked, you'll be partners of The Agency and Entertainment Management Worldwide."

I could tell this news pleased them.

They'd wanted this deal so fucking much.

I was happy I was able to make it happen for them.

"Do you have any questions?" I inquired.

"Not yet," Shane said. "But, as things get rolling, we might have a few."

I moved my hands to the end of the table. "Not a problem. I'll be here to answer anything that comes up." I stood and moved away from the chair. "Unless you have any concerns, I'm going to go finish a few things. I'll be back soon."

"We're good," Jayson said.

The other two nodded, agreeing with him, so I went down the hall to the service elevator, taking it down to the main floor. That was the same level Scarlett was on.

Once the door opened, I took out my phone to find Scarlett's last text, and then I began to type.

Me: Meet me in the ladies' restroom off the lobby. Ask the receptionist where it is. Knock once, and I'll let you in. Go right now.

The restroom I'd told her to go to was situated on the side of the lobby in a perfect spot. It was in a private hallway, so I could sneak in and out without my staff or Scarlett's partners seeing me. And it was the only restroom in the building that accommodated just one person; therefore, it had a lock.

I rushed toward the front of the building, knowing I didn't have much time, and I went inside the restroom. Once I flipped on the light, I locked the door behind me. Just as I finished washing my hands, I heard the knock.

Opening the door a crack, I saw that it was Scarlett, and I pulled her in, relocking it behind her.

"Hi—"

My lips crushed against hers before she even had a chance to get anything else out. *Fuck, I've missed her.* I cupped her face, holding her where I wanted her to be, my tongue hungrily sliding into her mouth. As her taste continued to fill me, I undid her belt buckle, and then I unbuttoned and unzipped her pants, pushing them down to her ankles.

I pulled my mouth away and said, "We have six minutes."

"Until?"

"My assistant goes into the lobby to get your group and bring you into my conference room."

"That's not much time."

I laughed as I got onto my knees. "It's plenty." I gripped the front of her lace panties and shredded the material until it was all sitting in my hand. Then, I threw them into the trash. "Put your cunt on my face." I bent my body, so I'd be the height she needed.

When she saw that she was able to straddle my mouth, she took a step forward and another until her pussy was hovering right over my tongue.

I didn't tease her.

I didn't go slow.

I didn't savor her clit like I had the last time my lips were on it.

Instead, I ate that fucking pussy as though it were the only piece of food that would ever be fed to me.

She moaned, "Oh my God, Hudson."

I made the same sound and growled, "*Mmm*."

It had been too goddamn long since my mouth was buried in her.

I hadn't just missed it.

I'd been craving it something fierce.

My tongue flattened, and I licked straight up the entire length, keeping my nose pressed to the top of her. Then, I switched it up and flicked horizontally and vertically. Once I established a rhythm, I plunged two fingers inside her.

"*Ahhh*, yes," she breathed. "You feel so good."

So did she.

And she tasted even better.

I mashed my tongue against her clit and finger-fucked her at the same time, picking up the speed in both, feeling her starting to tighten around my knuckles.

"Do you want to come?" I asked her.

"Yes."

"Then, I need you to tell me you'll have dinner with me tomorrow night."

She looked down at me. "You're fucking kidding me."

I gave her a few more licks to remind her of what I could do. "Not even a little." I twisted my fingers, driving all the way in. I bent them toward her stomach, finding her G-spot, and I circled around it.

"Ohhh," she sighed, especially as my tongue started to massage her again.

"Tell me you'll go to dinner with me, Scarlett."

"Hudson—"

"Tell me, or I'm going to leave you just like this."

"My God, you're relentless."

"Tell me," I growled.

"Fine, yes, I'll fucking go."

That was what I wanted to hear, so I rewarded her. I went harder, deeper, and when she began to fuck my face, I knew she was close.

"Hudson..."

"Come," I demanded. "Right now."

I sucked her clit into my mouth and thrust my fingers with even more power, feeling her upper body shudder above me.

As she was coming, I released her clit but kept my tongue on it, brushing it back and forth. And I continued to lick until she stopped moving.

With my mouth still on her, I glanced up, our eyes connecting.

"That was dirty," she said.

It was, but I'd gotten what I wanted.

"I'll make it painless," I told her. "At least until we get back to my place."

"I want more of what you just gave me. God, you're good at it."

I slid my fingers out and moved my lips off her clit. I got on my feet. "You make it easy. You have a gorgeous cunt."

She laughed as she fixed her clothes. "I'm so wet, and you've left me without any panties. I think that means I'm going to soak through my pants."

"When you get up from the conference room chair, I want to be able to smell your pussy on the seat."

I was going to check it after the meeting.

If I didn't get what I wanted, she would be punished.

I didn't go over to the sink to wash my hands. I wanted Scarlett's scent all over me for the rest of the day. But I took the dry fingers and pressed them on her cheek while I kissed the top of her head. "I'll see you in a few minutes."

As I left the restroom, I wiped my mouth and headed toward the back of the building to the service elevator. I took it to the floor where the conference room was located, and I joined my clients, taking the same seat I had been in eleven minutes ago.

We didn't have to wait long before everyone else joined us.

Once everyone shook hands and greeted each other, I waited for their attention to get started.

"Tina is going to pass out a folder to each of you." I watched my assistant go to the small table in the back of the room where she'd stacked the folders. She took them into her arms and began to hand them out. "Open the top flap and pull out the contents. We're going to start on page two, and I'm going to walk you through the entire packet. I'll explain every line you're required to sign."

My stare had moved around the room, but now, it was settled on Scarlett. She was sitting between Brett Young and Max Graham, and her eyes were locked on mine.

I hadn't had a chance earlier to appreciate how sexy she looked in her suit. How the shirt cut down to just the start of her cleavage and how the black jacket showed off her perfect frame.

Jesus, she's beautiful.

I was falling for this fucking girl and there was nothing I could do to stop it.

Nothing I wanted to do.

Because she was perfect.

Perfect for me, too.

I took my two fingers, the same two that had been inside her, and I grazed them across my bottom lip.

I could smell her.

I could taste her when I stuck my tongue out.

Scarlett blushed when she realized what I was doing.

She liked it.

She would like the sex swing we were going to use tonight even more.

And the breakfast I planned on cooking her in the morning since I was going to make her stay the night.

"If no one has any immediate questions," I said, "then go ahead and flip to page two."

FIFTEEN
HUDSON

NOW THAT THE merger between Entertainment Management Worldwide and The Agency had gone through and Scarlett had fulfilled her work obligations, she had a free night. I
knew what would happen if she came over. The same thing
had happened last night when she showed up at my house
after the seven of them had finished celebrating. I'd first tied
her to my massage table and used a riding crop on her body,
and then we'd played with the sex swing that I'd set up just
for her.

I wanted tonight to be different.

I wanted Scarlett to see how good we could be together.

So, I took her to dinner at one of my favorite restaurants.
The place was trendy, one of LA's hotspots that served dishes
that were old, authentic Beijing. Because I knew the owner, we
had the best table in here.

Scarlett sat across from me, my wine connoisseur sipping a
cabernet sauvignon from a Bordeaux glass, looking absolutely
beautiful. Her long hair hid those perfect fucking tits, and her

body was being hugged by the sexiest blue dress. Knowing those bare legs and spiked heels were underneath the table made me want to get on my knees and crawl beneath the tablecloth.

Even though she had initially been opposed to having a date, she'd let me pick her up from her hotel. She'd let me order several dishes for the table since the restaurant specialized in family-style dining. I had been shocked as hell when she even allowed me to choose the wine.

I hadn't asked what kind she preferred or if there were things she didn't eat.

I'd just ordered what I hoped she would enjoy.

And, because I assumed this was all a test anyway and that was the reason she had given in to me, I waited until after the waiter left our table to confirm, "How did I do?"

Her thumb traced the lip of the glass. "With what?"

"Tonight."

She brought the wine up to her face, her nose dipping into the opening to take in the aroma. "The wine is excellent." She took a sip and continued to hold it in her hand. "For dinner, I would have ordered one less appetizer and main course. We'll never even come close to finishing it all, but I know you wanted a variety in case I didn't like something. Fortunately, I like it all. As for the restaurant, it's one of my favorites. I eat at their Miami location quite often."

"I'd say I did good."

She smiled and nodded, and when a few seconds of silence passed between us, she said, "I've decided to extend my trip."

"Oh, yeah?"

She glanced around the dining room before her gaze returned to me. "With the merger, there's so much work to do, and Max left for Italy this morning. Someone needs to be here while he's away."

One day, I was going to be the reason she stayed.

She wasn't there yet.

But she would be soon.

"How much time are you going to give me, Scarlett?"

She drew in her bottom lip, her teeth rubbing over the left side of it.

Back and forth they went.

"I'm glad you're asking that question when your tongue isn't on my clit."

Mmm.

But that clit tasted so fucking good.

"I got what I wanted, didn't I?"

She took another drink of her wine. "You did, given the circumstances, but I don't promise that will happen again."

It was time to be honest and get some goddamn answers.

"What's it going to take to break you?"

"That depends on what you want."

My stare bore right through her. "I want you."

"You had me last night."

The thought of her on the sex swing entered my mind, the way she had straddled me on top of it, how I had swayed her into the air to ride my cock.

It had been a hot fucking night.

But, if it hadn't been about what she needed from me physically, then she wouldn't have come to my house.

"You've given me your body, Scarlett. I want to know when you're going to give me the rest."

"We've discussed this."

"We haven't discussed anything. You told me I lied and that, for now, you're comfortable with the way things are."

"That hasn't changed."

I studied her face, reading her in a way I hadn't before. "This isn't just about lying, is it?"

She looked down at the charger in front of her, staring at it for several seconds before her stare was back on me. "Part of it is that you live in LA, and I'm in Miami. I watched Max go through this for two years, same situation where his girlfriend was in California. You and I don't exactly have flexible jobs where we can spend half the month on the other side of the country."

"What's the other part?"

Her hands crossed over the center of the plate, her thumb brushing against the condensation on her water glass. "You have to understand something about me, Hudson. Lush is my place. It's my escape. Besides my home, it's where I feel the most comfortable. As a sexual submissive, I'm completely vulnerable in there. It requires a lot of trust—in myself, in my partner. On the night we met, I put that trust in you."

"And I lied."

She sighed. "Look, I'm not one to dwell on things despite how this might come across. What you did hasn't stopped me from spending time with you because I'm obviously doing that now. It's just, when I think about what our next step might look like, it crosses my mind."

"But you've thought about that step?"

"Yes." Her voice softened. "Of course I have."

I reached across the table and gently placed my hand over hers. "I know what I did was wrong, Scarlett, but you have to understand, it wasn't with malicious intent." I shook my head, wishing she weren't questioning my integrity. "How do I prove to you that you can trust me?"

She focused on the back of my hand, how my thumb was rubbing across her wrist. "You're already doing it." Emotion moved into her eyes. It was the first time I'd seen that from her. "And I'll admit, I like what you've shown me so far."

The waiter dropped off the appetizers, a dish of salt-and-pepper prawns and beef pancakes.

Scarlett put one of each on her plate and said, "Tell me how you see this working." She slid her hand out from under mine and picked up her chopsticks. "I mean, with the two of us so far away from each other."

I'd assumed she was done talking about us, so I was surprised she hadn't changed the subject.

But her question told me she was trying to piece it all together.

"I can break down the logistics and remind you that we have access to private planes and offices on the same coast, but you've already figured that out. You want to know if things between us will last while living on opposite sides of the country. My answer to that is yes. Why the hell not?" I put a few of the apps on my plate and took a bite of the pancake.

She finished chewing the prawn and set down her chopsticks. "You think it's that easy?"

"I don't think it's easy, but I don't think it should be an obstacle." I leaned in to get closer to her. "Listen to me, Scarlett; I'm not seeing anyone else, and let's be honest, I'm fucking crazy about you. I want more time with you—inside and outside of Lush." As I held her wrist, I felt her pulse start to increase. "When I'm not with you, I'm thinking about you, and I haven't been able to stop. Our sex is incredible, and you're as submissive in the bedroom as I am dominant. But that's not all..." Her pulse was hammering away even faster. "You're smart as hell, you're kind, beautiful, unbelievably stubborn. Don't you see how perfect we are for each other?"

Scarlett was a partner at The Agency with an equal share of ownership. She was her own boss and didn't need to ask anyone for permission. She had an office only a few blocks down from mine.

If she wanted to come to LA, nothing or no one could stop her.

But I wasn't going to bring that up. Not yet at least. I didn't want to freak her out and have her think I was already planning for her to move in to my place.

Although the thought had crossed my mind.

There was no way it couldn't have.

From the second my hands had touched her that very first night at Lush, I had known I wanted more with this girl.

Now that she was going to be spending some extra time in LA this week, I could get a good understanding of what that might look like.

SIXTEEN

SCARLETT

I'D SPENT a little over a week in LA, and when it was time to go back to Miami, I found myself dreading the flight. I wasn't sure I would have felt that way a year ago. But so much had changed, and there really was a need for me to be in California.

Our plan was to combine both LA offices. Since the one we had opened was larger, Entertainment Management Worldwide was going to move in with us. And, because we were acquiring a third location in Manhattan, it made sense for each coast to have their own finance department.

Every day that passed, I thought more and more that I should be the one running that department in LA.

The move was something I planned on discussing with Pepper when I went to her place for breakfast.

I'd known Pepper since college. We'd roomed together our freshman year, and we'd stayed close. When she'd opened the second location in Miami and started spending more time here, our friendship had grown even stronger. Out of all the women I'd met in LA and South Florida, Pepper was the only one I could call a best friend. And she was the only person I could be completely honest with because she knew this part of my life.

Because it was the morning and midweek, Pepper was at Lush, so that was where I went to meet her.

I entered the building through the back, using a private door that was reserved for employees. Down the hallway was a set of stairs that led to Pepper's apartment. She'd had it built when she opened the club, and she had the same setup at the one in LA, too. It wasn't where she lived; it was just a space for her to work in that was separate from the employees.

When I reached the door, I knocked, and she opened it within a few seconds, greeting me with a smile.

"It's been too long since I've seen you," she said, pulling me in for a hug.

"I know, and every time I was in LA these past few months, I was so swamped with work; I ended up sleeping at the office." I squeezed her even harder. "Promise we'll never let that much time pass again?"

"Promise." She released me, and I followed her into the kitchen. "What are we drinking? Wine?"

I looked at my watch to make sure I had the time right. "Pepper, it's not even ten. Plus, I have to go to work after this."

"Well then, how about a mimosa?"

I laughed.

God, I love this girl.

"Yes," I told her. "That's much better than wine."

She smiled hard and went over to the fridge. While she took out the orange juice and a bottle of champagne, I looked toward her living room. My favorite part of her apartment was the double-sided glass that ran the entire length of the room, overlooking the chamber downstairs. I was able to see the bar and the hallways that jetted off the center. I could even view the tables and couches and the people who were talking to each other.

The club was open all day, every day.

Whenever I found myself in her apartment, I was always so drawn to the glass. I loved being able to look down at the people below, at the chemistry that was building. I could feel the buzz of adrenaline all the way up here.

"I have some news for you," she said, taking two glasses out of the cabinet. She set them on the counter and filled them three-quarters full with champagne and a splash of juice. Then, she pushed one over to me. "I spent some time investigating Hudson Jones, trying to figure out how he'd gained entry to the club. Finding information on him wasn't as easy as I'd hoped."

"But you found something?"

She nodded.

There was a tightness in my chest that felt very much like nerves. I wasn't sure why I was feeling that way; it didn't make any sense. But I was certainly anxious over what she was about to tell me.

"Turns out, he dated Leanna, one of the girls who works for me. Leanna's older brother went to USC, where Hudson did his undergrad, and they were roommates. That's how Leanna met Hudson, and they dated all through college and while he attended law school. They grew apart after he graduated, and they broke up."

She paused, so I had to ask, "Is their breakup really part of this story?"

She smiled again. "No, I'm just telling you because I know you're curious."

"I'm that obvious?"

"Girl, you were obvious the second I told you I had news. Your ears perked up like a fucking bitch in heat."

I gulped down several swallows of my mimosa. Then, I took the hand that was holding the cold glass, and I pressed it against my cheek. "Keep going."

I wasn't sure how it was possible, but her grin grew even larger.

"Hudson had his assistant call Leanna, who has authorization to expedite memberships in extremely rare cases. This wasn't one, but Leanna made sure Hudson provided all the documents we require." She waved me into the living room, and we sat on one of the large couches where she turned her body toward me and continued, "In all honesty, had you not brought this to my attention, I probably never would have known. The problem is, our approval process is manual. Names aren't entered into our system until the member is approved. I don't track our waiting list; Leanna and the other girls do that. I only see who gets in. So, his membership never would have raised any flags had you not asked about him."

"During your research, did you find anything on him?"

She shook her head. "Not a thing. His background was clear, he has zero criminal history, he fits all the criteria we look for in a member—meaning he has money, status, and connections all over LA—and most importantly, he likes and practices the lifestyle that can be found downstairs. Oh, and he's single." She eyed me. "At least, I think he still is—unless that's changed in the last few days?"

"It hasn't." Everything she had just told me seemed so

straightforward. And, even though he'd told me I could trust him, I still had to check one last thing. "What about his middle name? Does he have one?"

She took her phone out of her bra, hit the screen several times, and said, "It's Andrew." She set it on the coffee table and looked at me. "So, if we break this down, technically, Hudson did nothing wrong. He provided what he needed to, he passed our requirements, and he paid the hefty membership fee. Leanna is the one at fault because she never should have used her authority to move his application through. Our waiting list is two years long. He should have waited like everyone else."

Hudson hadn't done anything shady, nothing that involved paying anyone off.

The only thing he'd done wrong was lie to me about his name.

But, when I really thought about it, anyone in his situation would have probably done the same.

He'd gone into Lush that night, thinking I would know who he was, that I'd be angry with him for being there and call him out.

He never thought I would look at him like he was just a regular member.

Except nothing about Hudson was regular at all.

The man was positively beautiful, certainly the most attractive guy I'd ever been with.

He gave me what I wanted.

Every time I asked for it.

He was so deliciously good at taking care of my body.

And, during the week I'd spent in LA, he had proven he was just as good at caring for me when I wasn't naked.

I turned to my side, my stare catching hers. "Did you fire Leanna?"

"No, but I've considered it. She helped someone gain access who was joining the club for the wrong reason. Maybe she didn't know his motive, maybe she did, but that's the part that doesn't sit well with me. I guarantee a safe and secure environment for my staff and members. Hudson could have jeopardized that." She glanced toward the glass wall and slowly back at me.

"What about Hudson? Are you going to revoke his membership?"

She studied my face before she said, "By the way you're looking at me, I'm going to take a guess and say you don't want me to."

"You're right; I don't."

She put her hand on my shoulder, squeezing it as she laughed. "So, you're having fun with him, but do you have feelings for him, too?"

Back in LA, I'd seen him almost every evening. We'd gone to Lush together several times that week. I'd spent the night at his house twice.

There were definitely feelings.

I couldn't keep denying them.

In fact, I really liked Hudson Jones.

He was irresistibly charming, protective, attentive, and extremely affectionate.

He was trustworthy.

The trust had just started off slow.

I downed the rest of my mimosa, my grin growing as large as hers, and I said, "I do. Serious ones."

SEVENTEEN

HUDSON

"TINA," I barked into the speaker of my desk phone, "I can't find the goddamn file on the Miller buyout."

"That's because, as of this morning, there is no more buyout."

I gripped the edge of my desk to pull my chair closer. "What the hell are you talking about?"

"Mr. Miller was arrested."

"For what?"

"Tax fraud."

I shook my head. "You have got to be kidding me."

So far, the buyout hadn't been a friendly one. In fact, it was one of the ugliest negotiations I'd ever experienced in all the years I'd been an attorney.

The buyer and seller were enemies.

And I'd bet my fucking balls that the opposition had had something to do with his arrest.

"Is the retainer gone?" I asked.

I heard her fingers clicking her keyboard. "According to

our records, Mr. Miller owes us for almost thirty-two hours, so at six hundred an hour, that's around nineteen thousand dollars."

"Send the bill to his wife."

"When I called her this morning, she was leaving for Europe and told me she would deal with it when she got back."

I smiled as I scraped a small mark off the glass top of my desk.

Mrs. Miller had better enjoy that trip. It was the last one she'd be taking for a while. Once the IRS started to dig, they were going to find a hell of a lot more than just tax fraud.

"I'll get in touch with her," I said. "Just get the bill ready and email it to me."

I hung up and clicked on Google, trying to find an article on his arrest. As I found several pages' worth, my private line rang.

I didn't bother to look at the screen before I hit Speaker and said, "Hudson Jones."

"Hello, Mr. Jones."

That fucking voice.

It didn't matter if she was ordering takeout or saying my name; she made everything sound so goddamn sexy.

"What can I do for you, baby?"

I checked the time. It was nine, which meant it was noon in Miami.

We usually texted during the day, and the only time I got to hear her voice was after she left work. And I could tell she'd had a few drinks. After about half a glass of wine, she was much more relaxed, and I could hear that in her tone.

Something was up.

"I just had a very interesting meeting," she said.

I swiveled my chair to face the window. The view overlooked the downtown skyline of Los Angeles. "Yeah? What about?"

"You."

I laughed. "With whom?"

"I'll give you a hint. I'm just leaving Lush."

My foot was tapping the floor, but her last statement caused it to freeze.

She was at fucking Lush?

And was talking about me? While another man was dominating her?

I wished she hadn't gone there without me. I just wasn't in a position where I could really dig into that unless I wanted to piss her off. But, man, things were finally good between us. She was slowly letting me in. We were talking every day. The one thing we hadn't talked about was whether we'd go to Lush without each other.

I hadn't been.

She obviously felt differently about it.

"I'm not going to fucking guess," I said. "Why don't you just tell me, Scarlett?"

"I was meeting with the owner to discuss your membership."

"That's why you were there?"

"Yes. Why? Did you think I had gone for a different reason?"

Jesus, that's a fucking relief.

But, now, the lightness in her voice told me she was testing me to hear how I'd respond.

It was time to play.

"Did you tell her how amazing I was?" I asked. "How she

needed to keep me around to make sure you were taken care of?"

"I was too busy trying to save your ass."

"*Mmm*," I growled. "Hearing that you had my back is so fucking hot."

"You want to know what isn't hot? Getting your membership revoked, which is what she wanted to do."

"On what grounds?"

"One, charming your ex-girlfriend into expediting your application to bypass the two-year waiting list. And two, joining a sex club for a reason other than to fulfill your sexual fantasy."

I laughed silently, the same way I would have if I were on the phone with a client. "Someone found out all my secrets. What was the verdict?"

She sighed. "It took some serious persuading, Hudson. To the point where you're going to owe me. Big."

"What do you want, Scarlett? My mouth on your pussy or for me to tie you to something and spank your fucking ass?"

Even though she took a few seconds to respond, I could tell from the noise she made that she liked the options.

"I want a weekend in Napa that includes your mouth and your palm."

I grabbed my dick, shifting it in my boxer briefs so that the tip didn't grind into my goddamn zipper.

She was making me fucking hard as hell.

"Traveling together?" I said. "That's a big step."

"I'm ready for it."

That was what I wanted, and I loved hearing it.

"Do you want to tell me when you're available?" I asked. "I'll have my assistant book it."

"I'm going to take care of everything. When I have the details, I'll let you know."

I turned toward the desk to grab a pen, clicking the top button nonstop with my thumb. "God, you're fucking dominant when you're not tied up."

"I can't fight you on that one," she said. "But the reason I'm planning this trip isn't because I want to control where we go and what we do and when we leave. It's because I want to do something nice for you. I think I owe it to you."

"You owe me nothing."

"But I do..." Her voice was so soft. "It's time I really show you how I feel about you, so let me do this, Hudson."

Tender was a side of her I hadn't seen.

I liked it as much as the others.

"I'm looking forward to it," I told her.

"I'm about to walk into my building. I'll call you later."

She needed to be rewarded.

And so did I, so I said, "When you do, make it a video chat, and I want you to be naked."

EIGHTEEN
SCARLETT

IT WAS JUST a coincidence that Max happened to be in Miami this week. Still, I couldn't have planned it more perfectly. This was a conversation I needed to have face-to-face while all three of my boys were present. Knowing their schedules were extremely tight, almost every minute of the day accounted for, I carved out a thirty-minute window for the four of us to meet.

When it was time, I walked down the hall and knocked on Brett's door, letting myself in. The three guys were already in there with an empty seat between Max and Jack.

"You guys are never this punctual," I told them as I went in and sat down. "Especially you, Max."

"Since we know something's up with you, we all came in here early to talk shit and try to figure out what the fuck you're going to tell us," Max said.

I turned to my right to look at him. "Are you serious?"

He laughed. "Hell no. We're discussing Manhattan and

how much work that's going to take, and we're deciding who's going to go up there to conduct the first round of interviews."

"Not me," I told them.

"I've been elected," Jack said. "It'll be over summer break, so Samantha and Lucy will come, and we'll spend a month or so up there."

Samantha was Jack's wife, and Lucy was their seven-year-old daughter. During the school year, the girls couldn't travel with him that much, and Jack hated it.

The room turned quiet, and I could feel all of their eyes on me.

When I realized I was staring at my hands, I looked up and met Brett's gaze.

"What's going on, Scarlett?"

The only way I knew how to address this was to put it right out there, so I said, "What would you guys say if I told you I wanted to move back to LA?"

"You'd better not be telling us that you're leaving The Agency," Max said.

My head shot to the right. "Leaving? No. I just mean, working out of LA instead of Miami."

"Jesus Christ," he groaned, wrapping his arm around my neck and pulling me close to kiss the top of my head. "I think you just gave everyone a heart attack."

Brett pushed away from his desk and leaned back in his chair. I could see the relief in his face, too. "Now that I know you're not leaving The Agency, I've got no issues with you moving out west. I'll just miss you like hell."

Being away from him and Jack was going to be so hard. We'd lived within five minutes of each other for our entire lives. So, living on opposite sides of the country was definitely going to take some getting used to. And it would require monthly visits at least.

"I'm excited as fuck that I'll have you out in LA with me," Max said.

I looked at Jack, as he was the only one who hadn't responded.

His eyes locked with mine. "I'm assuming this move has something to do with Hudson."

And there it was.

The giant elephant in the room.

"Why would you think that?" I asked him, although I was addressing all three since I knew they were thinking the same thing.

"Jesus, Scarlett," Brett said. "When it comes to you, you just tap right into us; you suck out all the details and then offer mouthfuls of unsolicited advice. But the second one of us tries to tap into you, you act like you don't speak fucking English."

My head tilted back as a laugh burst through my lips.

I couldn't help it.

He was right, and everyone in this room knew it.

"Guilty," I said when I stopped laughing enough to speak.

"You must think we're fucking idiots," Max said. "That the three of us can't read a guy's expression when he's looking across the table at a girl he just secretly fucked."

My hand went over my mouth after I said, "Max..."

I wanted to melt into this chair.

When it came to me, these weren't things we talked about.

"I know I'm not wrong," he added. "So, just admit things are going well with him and that he's weighing on your decision."

I looked at Brett and Jack to say something.

MARNI MANN

They said nothing, although I was sure they agreed with Max.

"For the last few months, I've been thinking about going back to LA. That office needs me more than Miami does, and I need it for me. But, yes, Hudson has helped with my decision. Spending more time with him will certainly benefit our relationship."

"Relationship, huh?" Brett said.

We hadn't named what we had together, but it felt like a relationship, and it was what we both wanted.

I shrugged as a smile tugged at my mouth. "He's perfect for me."

"He seems like it," Max said.

"It's nice to finally hear you admit it," Jack said.

"Don't get excited," I told all three. "You're getting no other information out of me. Ever. This was a one-shot deal."

"I don't think we can handle any more," Max said. "Telling the girl who's like a sister to you about the women you fuck is one thing, but hearing about the guys your sister fucks is just wrong."

"On so many levels," Jack said.

As I was shifting in my chair, recrossing my legs, Brett called out, "Hey." I glanced at him. "I'm proud of you."

"Why?"

"You learned from each of our mistakes, and I get the feeling you're handling this one differently than Vince," Brett replied.

"I am," I admitted. "But Hudson and I are so much more compatible."

"It's a good thing you're not waiting two years to live closer to him," Max said. "It gives your relationship a stronger chance, which you had to have learned from me."

"You haven't gotten pregnant; therefore, I'd say you learned something from me," Jack said.

I looked at Brett. His journey with James, a Hollywood actress, had been quite a rocky one, and a lot of it had happened in the public eye, especially because he was her agent.

I hadn't learned relationship advice from him.

What I'd learned was how to be a better human and friend.

All three had taught me that.

Brett leaned forward in his chair, resting his arms over the desk as he said, "We love you, and we only want you to be happy. But just let Hudson know, if he hurts you in any way, we're going to kick his fucking ass." His lips then moved into a smile, and he winked.

NINETEEN

HUDSON

IT WAS our second night in Napa, and we were staying in a private house that had been built into the side of a vineyard. Directly outside the windows were hills of grape vines. With the windows open, while we were cuddled in bed together, there was just enough moonlight for us to see the rows and rows of plants.

It was a gorgeous sight.

Scarlett couldn't get enough of it, and that was what I loved the most.

I held her against my bare chest, her face leaned against me as she looked out toward the night. My hand slowly ran over her hair, and I kissed the top of her head, leaving my lips there while I said, "When do you meet with the realtor?"

She'd been staying at my place since she moved to LA a week ago. Before she'd left Miami, she'd decided she was going to keep her condo there and get a rental in LA. She thought it was too soon to come live with me.

I was fine with it.

I knew she'd be in my bed every night even if she called another place home. I also knew her lease wouldn't last more than a year.

"The day after we get back." She traced her fingers over my abs. "She sent me about ten listings."

"Where are they?"

Her hand paused. "Hollywood Hills."

"I'm glad you listened to me."

I'd been telling her for the last week to look for homes in that area, the same section of the city where I lived. It would keep her close by and in one of the safer spots of town.

"I loved the Hollywood Hills when I lived in LA," she said. "I just couldn't afford it back then."

My hand moved to her back, and I rubbed the side of my thumb all the way down to the top of her ass and back up before I worked my way across her shoulders. "So, you're going to be looking for a place to live and restructuring the entire finance department for three offices."

"Technically, four until both LA offices merge. But, yes, please don't remind me; it's not going to be fun."

"That just means we're going to have to take more of these."

She tilted her face up, her lips now touching mine. "Every other weekend. That would be a dream."

"I'll make it happen."

She climbed a little higher, resting her face against my shoulder. "I love how good you are to me."

"You make it easy."

Her hand continued to draw over my skin while the both of us stared out the window.

Scarlett made silence easy. She made it tolerable.

But her voice was so sexy; I couldn't get enough of that either.

"Palm Springs," I said. "That should be the next trip."

"San Diego can come after."

"Then, we need to return to Napa."

"You really like it here?"

"I like how much you do, and that's what is important to me."

She nuzzled her face into my neck, and every exhale warmed my skin.

My arm tightened around her, and I pressed my cheek against her forehead. "It feels like I've been holding you for years," I whispered.

"I was thinking the same thing."

"You just feel so right. I don't want to let go."

"You don't have to." She reached higher, taking the pads of her fingers and brushing them over my lips. "Our start was so rocky; it's almost hard to believe we were there, and now, we're here."

"But it was sexy as hell."

I felt her smile. "That's true. That night with the flogger...*my God.*" There was another stream of silence, and then she broke it by saying, "Don't think I'm crazy, okay?"

"Never."

"It's just that, I know we're still learning each other and growing together as a couple, and we have so much ahead of us, but I feel something for you, Hudson." Her voice turned to a whisper. "It's a feeling I haven't had before." Her hand stopped moving, and she spread her fingers over me as though she needed to hold on. "Every day, I'm falling deeper and deeper in love with you."

I held her so tightly that she couldn't move, and I kept my lips against her as I said, "Baby, I love you, too."

EPILOGUE

HUDSON

I STOOD in front of Scarlett, looking down at her in the armless chair that I'd roped her to.

A flogger dangled from my hand.

There were marks on her body that showed every place it had touched her.

Everyone healed differently after a session. Scarlett, unlike any woman I'd ever dominated, just wanted a few seconds of rest and care, and then she always wanted my cock.

But, before I let her out of her restraints, I needed to hear a few words come out of that sexy fucking mouth.

"Beg for my cock," I demanded.

It wasn't just her voice I was after.

I wanted to watch the way her lips moved, to see the pleading in her eyes that was all for me and my dick.

"I want your cock, Hudson," she said, her lips wet, her eyes a little watery. "Please give me the pleasure I'm craving."

Hair was stuck to the sides of her sweaty face.

So fucking gorgeous.

"Louder," I barked.

"Please let me have your cock." She almost appeared breathless; she wanted it so badly. "I need it, Hudson. Please."

Mmm.

That was the noise I had been after.

Her head was pointed down, and she was looking at me through her long lashes.

She was such a good girl.

I moved closer and ran my hand past her forehead, stopping on the back of her head. I squeezed her hair between my fingers and used it to pull her neck back. "Say it one more time. Make me feel how much you want my dick in your cunt."

I kept her face steady as she opened her mouth, intensified her gaze, and said, "Please, Hudson. I need you inside my pussy. Don't make me wait for it. I want it now."

"Fuck," I moaned.

Before that happened, I needed something first.

I unzipped my pants and reached inside, leading my cock through the hole. Since I was already so close, I only had to aim it to the tip of her mouth. "Suck it."

She opened, and I glided in between her teeth.

"That's it," I said as her lips began pumping my fucking cock. "Take it deep."

Her tongue ran along the underside, and she swiveled back and forth to give equal pressure all the way around.

"Yes," I grunted. "Just like that, baby."

She was giving me so much suction, so much friction; she was making me want to come.

But it wasn't time for that yet, so I pulled out and moved behind the chair, carefully untying each of the knots. I made my way down her body, and when the ropes all fell to the ground, I helped her stand. Then, I wrapped a blanket over her shoulders and backed her up to the exam table that was in the center of the room.

Tonight, Scarlett was going to be my little patient, and I was going to do everything I could to heal her.

When her ass hit the table, I lifted her on top of the crinkled paper and rubbed her shoulders and legs. "You all right?"

She nodded.

"Tell me what hurts," I said with a smile.

She hadn't used her safe word, so I knew she wasn't in too much pain. What I was really asking was for her to role-play with me.

From the look on her face, she knew exactly what I was asking for.

"Hudson," she said in a voice that was much different than a few seconds ago, "I have this spot." She took her arm out of the blanket and pointed to her pussy. "It's down there, and it desperately needs your attention."

I put my hand on her calf and slowly worked my way up. "Tell me when I get close." I went past her knee and between her thighs. The higher I got, the warmer her skin was. And it was fucking scorching by the time I reached her cunt.

"There," she said when I brushed over her clit. "That's where I need you."

My finger dropped to her entrance and was immediately covered in a thick wetness. It was so slick, I had to stop myself from sliding in. "What about here?"

"*Ahhh*," she breathed. "Yes, there, too."

"I need you to get on your knees and point your ass toward the doctor. Can you do that for me like a good patient?"

"Yes," she said, sounding so fucking innocent.

MARNI MANN

She dropped the blanket from her body and turned around, crawling toward the top of the table.

Now that her ass was facing me, I stepped out of my pants, leaving my shirt on the floor right next to them. Once I was naked, I pulled her closer to the edge, and I soaked my fingers with spit from my mouth and rubbed them around her ass. When I knew it was lubed enough, I did the same to my cock, mixing it with her spit that was already there, and I gently drove in just a few inches.

"Hudson," she hissed.

I hissed right back at how fucking tight she was, how good she felt around my dick.

It didn't feel the same for her, but it would soon; she just needed to get used to it.

Slowly, I moved in a few inches more, and I continued sliding in until I was fully buried. I stayed still for several seconds, her ass pulsing around me.

When she pulled out to the center of my shaft and pushed back in, I knew she was ready.

"That fucking ass," I said as I took over, working all the way in. "Damn it, you're still so tight."

Within a few thrusts, she was screaming, "Harder!"

That was all I needed to hear.

I reared my hips back and bucked in. I felt her squeeze my cock when I was fully inside her. "Touch your clit," I ordered.

Her hand dipped between her legs, and I saw the movement of her elbow and forearm as she circled that hard little bud.

"Rub that fucking clit, Scarlett," I told her. My balls were tightening. A tingling feeling was spreading into my stomach. "Do you want to come?"

132

"Yes."

"Then, tell me you'll move in with me."

"Hudson, don't be ridiculous."

I increased my speed, nearing her toward that edge I knew she was already so close to. "Tell me, Scarlett. I want to hear that you're going to wake up next to me every morning."

She groaned. "I'll think about it."

"Not good enough."

I slid in and out several more times before she laughed and said, "Fine. I'll move in with you."

I knew I'd eventually get what I wanted.

Because I knew it was what she wanted, too.

I growled from her response and gave her even more power.

"Oh God," she moaned. "Hudson, *yesss.*"

Her thighs shook as the orgasm took ahold of her. Her ass quivered from the sensation, clenching me while I shot my first load. A burst of intense pleasure blasted through me each time I added to it until I fully emptied myself.

Just as I slid out, I turned her around and sat her on the table.

I set my hands on her face and pulled her close. "I'm going to clean you up, and then we're going home."

"*Mmm,*" she breathed, rubbing her nose against mine, her breath covering me. "I love the sound of that."

Have you read ...
Signed—*Brett's book*
Endorsed—*Jack's book*
Contracted—*Max's book*

ACKNOWLEDGMENTS

Jovana Shirley, I could never do this without you. I say that at the end of every book, and the words couldn't be truer. You're just incredible in every way, and I'm so grateful for everything you have done and continue to do. Love you. XO

Nina Grinstead, I love you more than anything. You're the most amazing publicist and friend. I can't imagine this journey with anyone but you.

Judy Zweifel, you rock my whole world. Thank you for everything, always.

Kaitie Reister, I love you, girl, so hard. You're my biggest cheerleader, and you're such a wonderful friend. Thank you for being you. XO

Letitia, I'm so in love with your work. You nailed this one, lady.

Kimmi Street, my soul sister, I love you more than anything.

Crystal Radaker, this book wouldn't have happened, nor would I have survived if it wasn't for you. You stayed right by my side during all those late nights, living off no sleep just so I could finish. That's love. Your friendship means more to me than you'll ever know. Love you so much.

Nikki Terrill and Andrea Lefkowitz, you two are incredible. Thanks for all your help, all the laughs, all the fantastic advice. I love having you two on this ride. XO

Extra-special love goes to Donna Cooksley Sanderson, Ratula Roy, Stacey Jacovina, Jesse James, Kayti McGee, Carol Nevarez, Julie Vaden, Elizabeth Kelley, RC Boldt, Jennifer Porpora, Melissa Mann, Pat Mann, Katie Amanatidis, my COPA ladies, and my group of Sarasota girls whom I love more than anything. I'm so grateful for all of you.

Mom and Dad, thanks for your unwavering belief in me and your constant encouragement. It means more than you'll ever know.

Brian, my words could never dent the amount of love you give me. Trust me when I say, I love you more.

My Midnighters, you are such a supportive, loving, motivating group. Thanks for being such an inspiration, for holding my hand when I need it, and for always begging for more words. I love you all.

To all the bloggers who read, review, share, post, tweet, Instagram—Thank you, thank you, thank you will never be enough. You do so much for our writing community, and we're so appreciative.

To my readers—I cherish each and every one of you. I'm so grateful for all the love you show my books, for taking the time to reach out to me, and for your passion and enthusiasm. I love, love, love you.

MARNI'S MIDNIGHTERS

Getting to know my readers is one of my favorite parts about being an author. In Marni's Midnighters, my private Facebook group, we chat about steamy books, sexy and taboo toys, and sensual book boyfriends. Team members also qualify for exclusive giveaways and are the first to receive sneak peeks of the projects I'm currently working on. To join Marni's Midnighters, click HERE.

ABOUT THE AUTHOR

Best-selling author Marni Mann knew she was going to be a writer since middle school. While other girls her age were daydreaming about teenage pop stars, Marni was fantasizing about penning her first novel. She crafts sexy, titillating stories that weave together her love of darkness, mystery, passion, and human emotions. A New Englander at heart, she now lives in Sarasota, Florida, with her husband and their two dogs. When she's not nose deep in her laptop, working on her next novel, she's scouring for chocolate, sipping wine, traveling, or devouring fabulous books.

Want to get in touch? Visit Marni at ...
www.marnismann.com
MarniMannBooks@gmail.com

ALSO BY MARNI MANN

THE AGENCY STAND-ALONE SERIES—Erotic Romance

Signed

Endorsed

Contracted

Negotiated

STAND-ALONE NOVELS

The Assistant (Contemporary Romance)

When Ashes Fall (Contemporary Romance)

The Unblocked Collection (Erotic Romance)

Wild Aces (Erotic Romance)

Prisoned (Dark Erotic Thriller)

THE SHADOWS SERIES—Erotic Romance

Seductive Shadows—Book One

Seductive Secrecy—Book Two

THE PRISONED SPIN-OFF DUET—Dark Erotic Thriller

Animal—Book One

Monster—Book Two

THE BAR HARBOR SERIES—New Adult

Pulled Beneath—Book One

Pulled Within—Book Two

THE MEMOIR SERIES—Dark Mainstream Fiction

Memoirs Aren't Fairytales—Book One

Scars from a Memoir—Book Two

NOVELS COWRITTEN WITH GIA RILEY

Lover (Erotic Romance)

Drowning (Contemporary Romance)